THE BUCCANEERS
OF
ST. FREDERICK ISLAND

LINDA MARIA FRANK

Publisher: Annie Tillery Mysteries, LLC

ISBN-13:
978-0-9989714-6-9

BOOKS BY LINDA MARIA FRANK

THE ANNIE TILLERY MYSTERY SERIES
1. The Madonna Ghost
2. Girl With Pencil, Drawing
3. Secrets in the Fairy Chimneys
4. The Mystery of the Lost Avenger
5. Making a Mystery with Annie Tillery: The Madonna Ghost
6. Secrets in the Fairy Chimneys, Second Edition

Available in paper, eBook, and audio at lindamariafrank.com

ACKNOWLEDGEMENTS

Accolades to my literary and technical assistant, Patricia Tergesen. This book came about because of her expertise, what she did and what she taught me.

My illustrator, Marianne Savage, is responsible for the beautiful and thought-provoking artwork, and for making the Buccaneers come alive visually.

The inspiration for this book was a childhood with a huge imagination.

My friends and fellow authors helped me to do the book because they thought I could.

And lastly, thank you, Nancy Drew. You made me a lifetime reader.

AUTHOR'S NOTES ABOUT THE STORY

WHERE DID THIS STORY COME FROM?

I was a wee tot of four when WII ended. As young as I was, I still have memories of what it was like in Middle Village, Queens, New York.

My dad was an air raid warden and besides running our small family florist business, he worked a shift at a defense plant called Accurate Brass.

When he went out on his air raid warden's rounds to check the neighborhood for violations, making sure no lights showed from someone's home where a blackout shade was carelessly left up, I held my breath. The threat was real since German U-boats had been regularly sighted off the coast of Long Island.

While my dad was outside my mom tucked my brother and me under a card table she'd covered with a thick blanket, providing us with a candle. Fire hazard, you say. This was the time before helmets, seat belts and car seats. We did all kinds of crazy things.

I recall being terrified that my father would not come home. It's hard to imagine the fear we felt when just across the Atlantic Ocean a war was raging. We felt vulnerable, and there were constant reminders all around us. Posters were everywhere. Uncle Sam Wants You! Buy War Bonds. And the one often repeated to this day, Loose Lips Sink Ships. Just to name a few. The subway was full of them.

My mom would take my brother and me from a nearby elevated train line to the South Ferry station at the tip of Manhattan Island where we would board the Staten Island ferry for a visit to my Aunt Lottie. I was so frightened as she carried me through the swirling mobs of civilians and uniformed men and women. My little fingers clutched her lambskin coat so fiercely they went through the fragile fur.

The challenge of food shopping and supporting the war effort had us waiting on lines to either use our ration book stamps to buy butter or meat, or to donate scrap metal and cans of grease drippings.

Letters came from my two uncles who were on Iwo Jima. They sent us a helmet (I don't know if it was American or Japanese). I learned to tie my shoes sitting in that helmet.

The War ended on VJ Day, Sept. 2, 1945. Mom woke me from one of her enforced naps during which I rarely slept. Firecrackers and shouting could be heard everywhere. There was joy tempered by the sadness of loss in those homes that displayed a gold star, the adults sobered by the tremendous sacrifice of lives. The United States suffered 400,000 casualties. As young as I was, I remember that the War was front and center in everyone's lives. Many a Sunday I sat on my grandfather's lap as everyone hovered around the radio, listening to Franklin Delano Roosevelt's Fire Side Chats, letting us know how things were going, and bolstering our courage. I didn't understand it all of course, but I did fully comprehend that something scary and important was going on.

Even the music on the radio seems to be seared in my brain. Without TV, radio was the way the world came into our homes. Edward R. Murrow reported from London amid the Blitz. H. V. Kaltenborn reported the news. And Frank

Sinatra started his amazing career. At four I didn't know who these people were, but their songs and voices, heard at a later time, were familiar.

Post-War America was where little six-year-old Linda started school in 1947. My memories of that period are what inspired this book. The Catholic School experience is still a subject of many reminiscences by friends.

One incident that is as clear as if it happened yesterday was the day my dad came to pick me up in the middle of a snowstorm. It wasn't the Blizzard of '47. That happened the day after Christmas so I would have been home. I was and it was a humdinger.

A knock came at the classroom door and Sister Superior ushered Dad into the room. Tall and handsome, dressed like a lumberjack, he nodded at our teacher, hat in hand, ever polite and proper. He collected me and my books and we climbed into his brand-new Dodge pick-up truck. The school was on a street with a slight incline. You can still see it from the Long Island Railroad as it makes its way from Forest Hills to Penn Station. The truck couldn't get traction on the icy snow-covered street and we slid sideways for a short distance. Dad pulled us out of the skid, and we went home.

Just like my parent's generation who survived the Great Depression, my generation was formed by surviving the crises of World War II. I created **The Buccaneers of St. Frederick Island** out of these memories, to capture for myself and others what it was like to be a kid with an adventure in a somewhat simpler time. I hope you enjoy it.

TABLE OF CONTENTS

ST. FREDERICK ISLAND

1947

SCHOOL DAYS

CHAPTER ONE

ON THE MOVE

How do those turtles do it? Pull their heads into their bodies? *Here comes Sr. JoAnn.* My head stubbornly remained on top of my neck.

If you think it's easy writing a note to the kid in the seat next to you when the rattling of Sr. JoAnn's rosary is announcing her slow walk down my aisle at this moment, you've never been to Catholic school. The room is silent. You can hear pen nibs scratching across the pages of our black and white composition books, leaving a trail of ink blots.

Pen nibs, you say. Ink blots? You won't believe this about the ink and the inkwell. Will you? We all learned to master a form of writing called the Palmer method. This is just another aspect of toughening the backbone here at St. BeSillius's. As I look at my permanently stained right middle finger, I wonder if I will be done in by something lurking in the ink and become St. Sprocket, patron saint of calligraphy.

The smell of chalk and old tempera paints barely covers the tinge of pine-scented urine coming from the old radiators. My mom went to this school and tells the story of kids leaning their wet behinds against the radiators to let their underwear dry if they had an accident. Going to the bathroom in those days was a privilege reserved for the Pope. Thank God things have changed, and St. BeSillius has hired a nurse, and given her an office where this kind of thing could be taken care of.

A floorboard squeaks. I hear the faint clink of keys as if Sr. has reached into the stygian depths of her pocket for something. I slide my ruler over the words I've just written and peer cautiously from the side of my vision trying to locate Sr. JoAnn. My stomach bunches. She is reading Eddie O'Malley's entire page. Eddie's not one of us, so there is nothing out of the ordinary to see in his notebook.

My page is full of writing, but not what I think I want Sister to see. So far, I've jotted a list: LOOK FOR CLUES, including the narvex, the sacristy, the side entrance, the choir loft, and the bushes around the church. I've signed it, Sprocket.

Sprocket? Is that a Christian name? Of course not, silly reader. We all have code names to protect the guilty. We are the Buccaneers of St. BeSillius School, a secret society dedicated to solving the mysteries and misdeeds of our little parish school and the island where it's located.

Uh-oh. Here she comes. If I rip the page out and crumple it, she'll just grab it. And, I'll have to explain why there's nothing on the page, in longhand mind you, about the characteristics that would have made George Washington a good Catholic, if only he had known better.

George was an Anglican having once been a colonial loyal to the King of England, also a George. But that's another story.

Eddie, not the sharpest pencil in the box, is getting the Spanish Inquisition treatment about his lack of inspiration on the topic. I wonder if the nuns get a special course in interrogation techniques.

Eddie, I love him dearly, is buying me time. Could I quietly turn the page and jot a quick sentence or two? I pick up the notebook and turn the page, knocking a pen full of ink onto the floor along with the ink well. As you can imagine, this was not a silent maneuver. Sr. JoAnn, Eddie and the whole class look at me. I feel my face burn. I get up to clean the mess and knock the composition book on the floor with my note showing plainly on top. Sister reaches for it. I'M DEAD!

The fire drill siren shrieks. Sister turns to move the class to the fire exit, and I kick the composition book under the desk. It obliges me, closing with a snap.

"I'll clean this later, Sister." I smile.

"And I will be checking your essay." She smiles back.

"Yes, Sister," I say, noting that the proverbial glove his been tossed onto the floor like they did in those ancient duels. I file past her.

✳✳✳

Are you wondering why a bunch of Catholic school kids are searching for clues in what looks like a church and the yard around it?

Let me digress for a bit and fill you in on some details about why we are listing clues and what all this skullduggery (Great word, isn't it?) is about.

Well, before I fill you in on what happened when we found those clues, let me explain who we are. We call ourselves The Secret Crime-Stoppers of Sts. Christopher and Michael, but I wanted a shorter title like Buccaneers of St. BeSillius. I thought calling on both St. Christopher and St. Michael was pushing the envelope of sponsorship. And who even knows who St. BeSillius is? So, just think of us as the Buccaneers.

For the past year, our class has been raising money for a class trip to visit seven churches on the mainland and distribute toys to the children's day care centers in those parishes. We did bake sales, car washes, leaf-raking, snow shoveling. We cleaned attics for old ladies, cut lawns and pulled weeds. Some ill-informed parents even let us do fence-painting. Don't worry! Those shrubs will come back in a year or two.

A whole year of those earnings went into the fund. We kept it in the vestry. That's the room behind the altar in the church where the priest keeps his vestments. Get it? Vestry, vestments? The box with the money disappeared the day Father Felix was supposed to open a bank account for us. We never got the money back, never found out who did it, and we're pi….. Whoops! Sorry. I'm just angry. Not mad. Sister Priscilla said that mad means crazy. Well, she hasn't been paying attention to her students.

Anyway, even though the sisters and priests said we should offer it up to God. I'm not sure what that means, the money or the cursing we did. And, we should learn a lesson. Next time lock it up! And where were we supposed to lock it up? It was in the vestry! With Father Felix, the parish priest!

This didn't go down too well with some of us, and one night last summer at our club house which is just a shack on the beach, we decided to form our own little PI group, that's Private Investigator. We voted on and accepted our official title, Buccaneers of St.Besillius. Look. You can't beat our creativity in naming the group. We even researched St. BS. She's the patron saint of mimes.

As we gathered around the fire, we wrote up a charter including the following:

- ✔ Each member is sworn to secrecy, under pain of... what? Oh, I don't know.

- ✔ All clues are to be shared by everyone.

- ✔ All communications would be done using our code names. Mine is Sprocket.

- ✔ Our meeting place would be the old fishing shack on the beach.

We made a list of our code names.

Lily code name Sprocket, all around smarty, leader, that's me.

Ryan: code name Bletch, general genius.

Frank: code name Wingnut, mechanical genius, and a bit dippy.

Leon: code name Snap Shackle, math genius, can put two and two together.

Amalie: code name Ratchet, electronic surveillance, or just plain snoop, meaning she can use a camera.

And so, the story begins.

CHAPTER 2

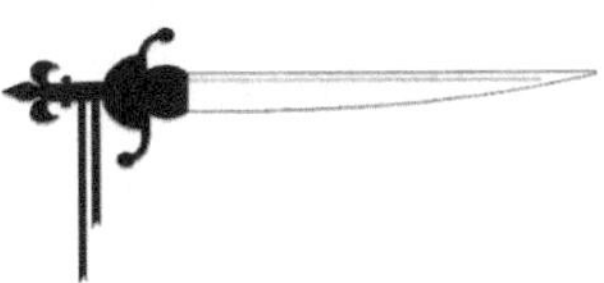

TALKING DURING A FIRE DRILL

I pulled up my knee socks for what must have been the tenth time today, and hurried after the other kids, moving like cockroaches when someone turns the light on.

I caught up to Wingnut who was practicing a skill every Catholic School kid learns, that of communicating in a ventriloquist's voice.

"Did Sister see your note?"

"No, but it was a close call. I knocked over the ink well and the notebook is soaked in ink. The message is obliterated".

Thank you, Saint BeSillius, I prayed.

St. BeSillius, as I have mentioned, takes care of mimes, who communicate through body language, gestures, and facial expressions. Even though the students here at St. BS's don't take a vow of silence, the results of the discipline our teachers impose, is that it helps you to be a mime if you want to get a message across to your friends.

Perhaps you'd like a little background? The school at St. BS was housed in the oldest building on the Island of St. Frederick, or Fred as we affectionately call our plot of earth surrounded by water. Legend has it that this building was erected pre-American Revolution by the pirate, Jon Buccleigh. One would think that a pirate would be foot loose and not anchored to one place. Not, Buch-O as he was known. According to the legend, he had free run of the coast here.

You need to understand that Fred is still isolated. It's a forty-five-minute ferry ride to get to the main island that is connected to the mainland by a bridge. Back in the 18th Century a forty-five-minute ferry ride of today would take hours. The island is smothered in fog five days out of seven. The currents are tricky too. Many a kayaker or canoer, even small power boats are rescued by the Coast Guard or one of our plucky boatmen every year.

Getting back to the school building. It was authentically dated at 1770. It's old. Several attempts have been made over the years to reconstruct, modernize, and otherwise improve the place.

It has its charm, and of course, its nooks and crannies give rise to all manner of ghost stories and pirate plots, kidnapped damsels, and unexplained disappearances. How'my doin' so far with St. BS's history?

There was a tale about one of the Sisters disappearing in 1843. It was even in the newspaper. The staff here at the school never talk about it, but my mom and I looked it up in the library on the main island. The nun was later found. She had run off with one of the fishermen. No wonder her story was one of those best kept secrets. By the way, the main island is called Main Island. I wonder whose amazing imagination came up with that one.

But as we left our classroom, the corridor in front of us, shining like a newly groomed ice rink, led us to the massive front door. If I closed my eyes, I could see the door creak open and Buccleigh's men dragging loot across a drawbridge into their castle lair.

The shiny floor reflected the stained glass that decorated the high windows above the classroom doors. The smell of floor wax scented the air along with beeswax candles and incense drifting from the chapel. Saints and the Virgin occupy little alcoves from one end of the hall to the other.

The all clear gong echoed from the main office and we headed back to class.

"What's the plan? We'll have to pass it along the usual route to get everyone on board," Wingnut said, not a muscle of his mouth moving.

I thought about this. The usual route required some messages secreted behind the poor box in chapel, under statues of the Virgin and Saints, and in blackboard erasers which had to be clapped outdoors to remove the chalk dust. Sister JoAnn never seemed to notice the increase in piety or the fervor to do a good deed, or maybe she was onto us, and hadn't figured out exactly what it was she was onto.

"Forget it. I haven't got my plan together yet, and we meet on Friday anyway. Leave it at that."

Best not to create any more suspicion at this point, I thought. *We are going to get to the bottom of this!*

Wingnut seemed to shrink by two sizes like a deflated balloon at this turn of events.

"Hey, call me tonight. Help me with the plan, okay?" I offered.

Wingnut re-inflated, and we did a thumbs-up. We rushed to catch the rest of the class, melting into the crowd. Wingnut, who deserves his nickname, was snorting, shoulders jerking, like he was having some sort of a fit.

"What's up with you, Wingie," I said. "You look like you've got a spider in your shirt."

"I just remembered a story my Dad told me." He poked me hard. "Oh-oh."

Sister Superior was staring at us with that death-ray look (I'm not kidding. You could see the yellow light streaking from her eyes.) that promised dire consequences if you continued down the road you'd just chosen. Foolishly, of course.

"Tell ya later," Wingnut whispered.

"There is NO talking before or AFTER a fire drill."

"Yes, Sister Superior," we chorused, and scurried off, hoping to escape any remedy she had for breaking fire drill rules. A quick glance over my shoulder revealed Sister JoAnn and Sister Superior frowning and pointing to us.

Sister JoAnn and Mother Superior (no one knew her real name) belonged to an order of nuns that chose to keep their original habits. I guess they figured that the habits weren't bad habits. My sense of humor comes from living on this island.

The long black old-fashioned dress was equipped with large rosary beads. A broad white collar adorned the neckline of the dress. It made me think of Puritans or Pilgrims. The whole effect was topped off with a bonnet that made the two sisters look like Lil' Miss Muffit. The habit definitely set the nuns apart.

Sister Superior was very tall with a long narrow face. She always appeared stern, girding herself for the next Crusade. Sister JoAnn was small and round-faced and pretty. She was the more approachable of the two, unless, of course, you crossed her.

But with their heads together, speaking in whispers while eying Wingnut and me, I felt my stomach cramp, remembering their advice to forgive and forget. It fell on deaf ears. That was not our plan. I think they suspected something, so we would have to be careful.

Wingnut and I exchanged a final knowing look and I headed back to clean up the ink, all the while trying to push my anger down, so I could think clearly and plan our moves. I wasn't about to forgive and forget, pray for the soul who did the evil deed, and neither were my friends. We were going to find out who stole the money we raised to buy toys for needy kids and get that money back.

CHAPTER THREE

SABOTAGE

The rest of the day went as usual. George Washington was deemed to be a great candidate for Baptism into the Roman Catholic Church, a moot point since he was dead. Sister JoAnn put the kibosh on any discussion of whether the Father of our country made it to heaven or not.

The dismissal bell found me high tailing it home. I walked in on what looked like a Mexican stand-off between Boots, my Scotch terrier and Fish, our Tabby cat. The radio played "Little Brown Jug" in the background, a catchy Glenn Miller tune. Mom loved Glenn Miller. She said it reminded her of Dad.

Boots positioned herself between Fish and Fish's food dish. She crouched, facing Fish, rear end up in the air, stubby little black tail wagging. A low gurgling little groan announced she was ready to challenge the cat to a fur-flying, caterwauling, barking melee.

Fish, her tail expanded to resemble my mom's feather duster, executed two swift moves, vaulting onto the kitchen counter, and leaping to the top of the fridge's round compressor.

From that lofty perch, she proceeded to lick her tail into a more manageable style, all the while glaring down her cute orange nose at Boots who was now running around in circles in frustration. This little tableau was repeated so often that I was beginning to believe Boots was either retarded or suffered from canine dementia.

"Wanna treat," I called, clapping my hands.

Before you could say Jon Buccleigh's teeth, my two little buddies sat at attention at my feet.

Slipping off my backpack, I jiggled the treat jar. Behind me eight little paws did a tap dance on the tile floor. Treats accepted, truce declared, peace reigned in our home, Windalee Cottage. The radio went to another Glen Miller tune. Mom really loved this guy's music.

The door to the porch that faced the beach on the other side of the house banged shut.

"Mom?" I called.

Her bare feet slapped along the tiles as she made her way to the kitchen.

"Lily. I'm glad you're home."

I didn't like what I saw. Her hair clung to her face in sweaty ringlets. Her sweater and pants were streaked with some black stuff. And she looked at me with an expression that said, "I'm so sorry your goldfish died." Only I haven't had a goldfish since the one whose demise she told me about died when I was five.

"Mom?" My knees were beginning to feel watery. If my heart hadn't stopped, it would be pounding."

"What's wrong, for Pete's sake. You look like you've seen a ghost!"

"Oh, Honey! She was coming at me with open arms ready to hug me."

"What is it, Mom. You're scaring me!"

"There was a fire today, just before lunch, and it was your beach shack."

The beach shack was our clubhouse. The Buccaneers held our meetings there.

"Whaa . . . Who? Do the firemen know what happened?"

"They think it was a homeless person who was living there during the day when you and your buddies were in classes."

I pulled out a kitchen chair and sat down hard.

Could this be connected to the stolen money, I wondered.
"I know the homeless beachies, and I don't think anyone of them would set a fire so carelessly. It's never happened before."

Things were beginning to make nooooo sense. The first thing I needed to do was to figure out how to get the Buccaneers together, and where, so we could get down to business. This was spinning out of control. So was my head.

"Well, Lass. I've been looking. I found this." He opened a waxed-paper sandwich wrapper and showed me four cigarette butts, Camels.."
I reached for them, but he closed the paper wrapper and the package disappeared into his pocket before I could protest.

"I'll be holdin' on to these," he said.

CHAPTER FOUR

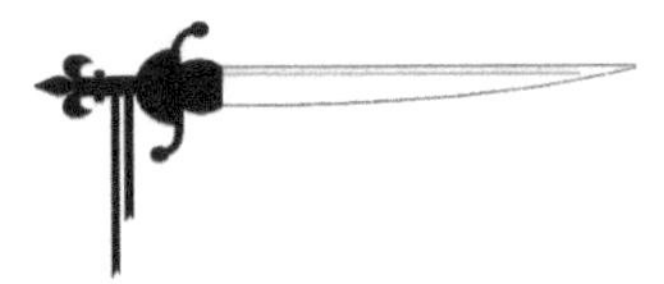

THE CRIME SCENE

"Lily!"

I heard Mom's voice from some echo chamber.

"I'm getting up. Stop shaking me for Pete's sake!"

"You fainted," Mom announced as I picked my head off the kitchen table.

"I have to get to the Buccaneers, Mom. Can you help?"

"You need to tell me who they are, and I can use the telephone chain from the mother's auxiliary to contact the mothers who will tell their kids.”

“No! No! No! Mom, I don’t want every Tom, Dick and Harry in on this. Everyone will be out there checking out the fire, as it is. Evidence will be destroyed. Sorry. I’m not thinking straight.”

I’ll call Win-uh-Frank and have him use our own secret messaging system.”

“Which is?”

“If I tell you, it won’t be a secret system anymore.”

Mom glared. I looked at my shoes.

Since my dad died in a boating accident two years ago, Mom has begun to lean on me, wanting to know every little detail of my life. My choices are telling her what she wants to know, tell her I need to have some privacy, or just lie. A mental picture of my guardian angel weeping in the corner, pointing a finger at me, and calling me a liar, tries to lodge in my brain. I banish it. I have work to do.

"Mom, it's no big deal. It's just a way to get in touch on this very insulated island. I can't tell you without breaking trust with the other Buccaneers."

She nodded, looking resigned and rejected.

"Mom?" She looked up.

"I love you, but everyone needs something of their own."

She nodded again. "Do you feel okay?" she asked, getting back to business.

"I think so."

She left me to do what I needed to do. The telephone sat on a small table in the hallway off the kitchen. I pulled out the even smaller chair Mom had restored from a dumpster-diving expedition on Main Island.

All the phones on Fred were on a party line, but you could call a person's number, and if no one else was on the line, the call would be private. We had a way of getting around that. Code, of course.

I dialed Wingnut's number, waiting for the rotary dial to return before sticking my finger in the next number's round hole and rotating the dial again.

There's gotta be a better way to do this. Anyone ever think of push buttons?

Wingnut picked up and I heard three other clicks, a dead give-away that others were listening in. Friend or Foe? Who knows?

"The weather in Bermuda is approaching gale force, Beaufort nine."

We used the Beaufort scale to indicate what level of emergency we were facing. Nine is the ultimate emergency.

Wingnut hung up and would then call the next number in our chain.

Mom returned with clean clothes and a towel wrapped around her head. She was very pretty, even with the tired frown lines between her brow.

"I'm going to take a look at what's left of our shack." I grabbed a jacket, but Mom pulled me back.

"It'll be dark before you can get back. Wait until tomorrow. I don't like this situation one bit."

"I can't, Mom. What if someone comes in and destroys evidence? If the fire is arson, that's exactly what they'll do. I heard that arsonists are known to linger around their fire or visit the scene later."

"Where does she get this stuff," Mom muttered.

She dropped my arm with a sigh. "All right, but I'm going with you." Taking the towel off her head and cramming a wool cap over her damp hair, she grabbed keys, locking the door as we left.

She was upset. We never lock doors here, I thought.

The path that would take us to the shack was easily accessed from behind our house. It led along the beach. It was quiet, a fog gently rolling off the surf as it did almost every day in late afternoon. Dog walkers dotted the line along the surf.

A few minutes into our walk I picked up the odor of charred wood. Mom said nothing and I was glad. My brain churned, trying to make sense of all the unanswered questions.

Was it an accident? I didn't think so.

If it wasn't, who did it?

Was it related to the stolen money?

How was I going to protect the ruined club house until tomorrow? Especially, since we had school.

The smell got so strong that I looked up expecting to see the smoldering ruins. A figure was appearing and disappearing among the burned timbers that remained upright. I ran toward the sight and yelled at the top of my lungs, "Hey, stop. Who are you?"

The figure came out of the ruins and as I got close enough, I saw who it was. It was Sebastian (Sibby) Fintail, one of the local Fredites who lived off the land and the sea. He inhabited one of the other shacks used by beachies, as we called them, folks like him. He was a character, really eccentric, but a good guy. He knew about the Buccaneers, having admitted to listening in on our meetings.

"Sibby! Find anything interesting?"

"Not yet, Spro…er…Lily," he said, quickly deciding not to use my code name, in case Mom was not in on our little "organization."

"I am that sorry that you lost your clubhouse."

"Did you see anything? Do you know how this happened?" I asked, hoping he had. The beachies were the best observers around. They were always out and about and saw everything.

Sibby was probably 40 to 45 but looked older. He was so weather beaten. Since he didn't serve in the war, I knew he was older than my dad, but not an old man.

He was wearing his yellow foul weather pants, held up by suspenders, over a black and red plaid shirt. Dark green sea boots completed his nautical ensemble. His hair was sandy brown with gray and white sprinkled all over. His blue eyes peered out from pockets of reddened wrinkled flesh. His face was always bright red from wind and sun. As burly as he appeared, he was always neat and clean-shaven showing a deeply dimpled chin.

That clean shave reminded me of my dad, smooth, but with a hint of a coming new beard. I tried to remember that face. I had to look at some photos we had of him to really remember. I sure wish he were here now. He'd have something to add, a suggestion, a plan, a shoulder to lean on. I looked over at Mom. I knew she must be thinking the same thing.

Sibby was looking at Mom too. I couldn't read that look.

"Well, Lass. I've been looking. I found this." He opened a waxed-paper sandwich wrapper and showed me four cigarette butts, Camels.

"Any of your clan smokers?"

"Not that I know of." I reached for them, but he closed the paper wrapper and the package disappeared into his pocket before I could protest.

"I'll be holdin' on to these," he said.

"But . . ."

"Not these butts and no other buts, Lassie. I think something is real off here, and I'm stronger than you."

He had a point, but I wish he would lay off the Lassie bit. I keep thinking of the dog, not Scottish girls.

Arf, played in my mind's ear.

CHAPTER FIVE

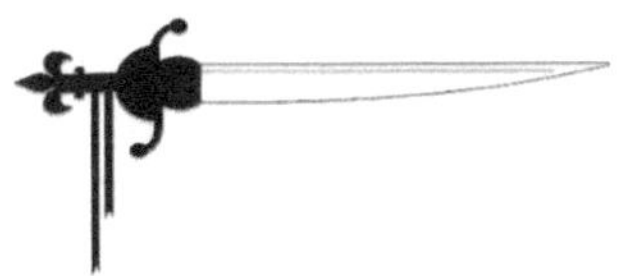

SIFTING THROUGH THE ASHES

"It'll be dark soon. I wanted to get back to the house while it's still light out. This whole thing makes me nervous. What if it is an arsonist and this is just the first fire in a series?" Mom said this while pacing around the burned-out shack, kicking little puffs of sand here and there.

I could see that she was agitated. She had been looking around, rubbing her hands together. Taking care of everything since Dad's death was tough on her.

She kept the island's only newspaper, *The Foghorn,* going, relying on the good will of past contributors and with a few clever ideas of her own. I thought the best one was a medical column that had recruited a local Native American healer to provide advice. Many islanders had faith in her.

"Mrs. Dawes, I'll take you and Lily back home," Sibby declared.

Hmmmm. This wasn't the first time Sibby seemed to want to help Mom out.

Her shoulders dropped, and she looked up at Sibby, "Thank you. I would feel much better if you could look around the house with us to make sure nothing seems off."

Sibby smiled. A very bright smile indeed. "It's my pleasure, Ma'am. Don't want anything to happen to you or Lily here."

"Please call me Becca, Sibby. Ma'am is too formal."

It was settled. With one last look at the rubble left by the fire we headed to the surf line walking back to our house with our stalwart protector. Sibby, hands jammed in his pockets, humming, "Comin' Through the Rye".

But soon, Mom and Sibby chatted, "How are your new ideas for the newspaper going, Becca?" Sibby, by the way, was Mom's printer for the paper, *The Foghorn*. Mom's the editor in chief, owner, and chief cook and bottle washer.

"The new health column is very popular. Tabitha Blue Smoke is giving some simple Native American remedies that will go over big here, since they don't require doctor or pharmacy. I've gotten several more subscription requests. My next idea is to run installments on a weekly basis of local myths, histories, and folk lore from the residents." Mom was really warming to the subject." I also want to have the sports team captains write the recap of games and especially season finales."

"Aye, all good ideas, Becca. I will have to dig through my clabber to see if I can give you a story to make your readers hair stand on end."

Where in the name of St. BeSillius did he get the pirate talk? I will have to ask him. If he gets a parrot and a peg leg, I won't be surprised.

But Mom laughed and seemed to relax.

She and Sibby chatted about *The Foghorn.*

"I had a bad catarrh two weeks ago, and I tried some of that boneset tea in BlueSmoke's health column. Dang, if it didn't work."

"What the heck is a catarrh? It sounded fatal to me."

"Oh, it's just a cold, Lily."

"Then why do you have to set your bones to get rid of it?"

This native healing is losing me.

"It's just an old-fashioned name for the herb that helps cut the mucous production in a cold," Mom explained.

"I see. A snot-stopper!" I snorted at my own joke.

"Ugh! Lily!"

Sibby guffawed.

What a silly word for a rude laugh.

This fascinating conversation made the walk back to the house go quickly. I looked up at Mom's quick intake of breath. The screen was hanging off the kitchen window, and the screen door was slightly ajar.

CHAPTER SIX

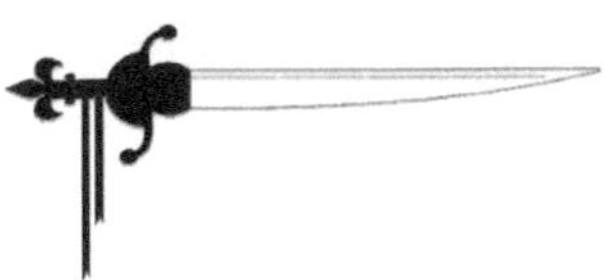

WINGNUT FAILS CRIME SCHOOL

"Stay here. I'll check the inside. I don't like this at'll." Sibby hunched his shoulders and headed for the kitchen door. It was unlocked.

"I locked it when we left," Mom whispered.

Sibby disappeared inside the house. I couldn't stand it. I crept up to the door, Mom just a step behind me. There was a loud crash inside the house, followed by furious barking and the yowling of our cat.

A body pin-wheeled out of the kitchen door, knocking into us. Mom grabbed at its shirt, and I tripped him. It turned out to be a him. He fell, and I sat on him.

Sibby came barreling out of the house, followed by a barking Boots and a howling Fish.

Mom pulled the jacket off the face of the intruder.

"Wingnut!" "Frank!" We shouted in unison.

Wingnut groaned.

"What are you doing, breaking into my house?" I screeched, shaking him furiously. "You scared us; you jerk!"

Wingnut's judgment was rarely spot-on. "Well?"

"You weren't home. I figured I'd just slip in, get tonight's homework, and slip out. You just arrived in the middle of it. Could you get off me, please?"

"Through a locked door! I shouted. "You'd just slip in?"

"Oh, ah, I picked the lock," Wing confessed, looking at his shoes. "Please get off," he wheezed.

"Oh, sure," I said rolling off and thinking, being an eighth-grade girl, I probably outweighed this eighth-grade boy by ten pounds.

Sibby, who looked like an approaching tornado, glared at Wing. "I coulda hurt you. It was too dark to see who it was in there."

"I'm sorry. I gotta get home to watch my baby sister," Wing said backing up, ready to flee. "Mom's helping out at the lighthouse tonight."

"Your nose is bleeding. Mom said. "Come inside and I'll clean you up, so your mom doesn't have a heart attack when she sees you."

"I'll check the house and walk him home," Sibby offered, "After I see you lock up."

"Thanks." Mom shot Sibby a grateful glance as she pushed Wing into the kitchen and ran the cold water to clean him up.

I knew it wasn't homework Wing was looking for, but I didn't know how to find out what, with Mom there. I stood behind Mom and gave Wing a *what gives* body message. He nodded slightly, and I ran to my room. Outside of my room being tossed a bit, everything looked normal. Mom finished with Wing, and the two of them left with Sibby's final warning. "Keep the doors locked, and I'll check in the morning."

Sibby's shack had no phone. We couldn't call him for help. Maybe smoke signals?

CHAPTER SEVEN

ISLAND MEDICINE

Safely locked inside, a steady rain set in as we prepared supper.

"Mom. I was just thinking about the people on this island. Who would want to do this, burning our shack? Who stole our money? You think it might be Mrs. Blue Smoke?"

Mom turned from the stove and stared at me. "What brought that on?"

"Dunno. She just popped into my head." Sibby's praising of the cure that the Native American healer featured in the last column made me remember that she was the mother of one the students at Saint BS. Her name was Tabitha Blue Smoke, and her daughter, Janet. I mulled these names over, and realized Tabitha is an old English name, Blue Smoke is Native American, and Janet is Scottish. Wonder what a family tree search would do with that?

"Tabitha's and Janet's family and the North Breeze tribe have been living on Fred, well forever. Before the present inhabitants came, St. Frederick Island was never attractive to the settlers of the 1700's. Too remote, ugly weather, and I think they were afraid of the Native Americans. Main Island was a better choice."

"So, what brought the inhabitants who live here now to Fred?"

Mom continued. "Many are descendants of the tribe. Some are *free spirits* whose families have lived off the farms they wrested from the forest here and the seafood that is plentiful in the waters around the island and the near-by ocean. Others, like Daddy, who worked for the State Fish and Wildlife Service were assigned here. We loved, love, it here."

"There were no actual houses owned by the state for us to live in. We were able to claim one of the abandoned beach shacks and turn it into a reasonable place to live."

I knew the history of St. BS. It was claimed by the Roman Catholic Church in a bankruptcy deal. It was originally slated to be an old age home for nuns, but complications arose when residents who had children were not sending them to school and the State decided it was a perfect location for a school. Because, let's face it, it would be impossible, given the forty-five-minute ferry ride to send little kids to school on Main.

St. BeSillius became the logical place for a school, and a small clinic. The Church made a deal with the state to give the facility "not for profit" status, including all the tax exemptions and other goodies involved. In other words, it would cost the Church a Peter's pence (pardon the pun) to run the buildings as church, school, and clinic.

But I digress. Again.

"Well pop her right out of your head," Mom said rousing me from my musings. "And don't go floating that theory with your friends, either."

"Mrs. Blue Smoke is an LPN, a licensed practical nurse. She combines traditional and herbal medicines and is an asset to the communities here on Fred."

"Janet Blue Smoke is in my grade, but not in my class."

She went on. "There are a couple of Blue Smoke families. They are all part of the same clan though."

"How did you get her to do the column in *The Foghorn*," I asked.

"She came to me. She's trying to get more folks to try buying and using her herbal cures. Let's face it. Many of the Native Americans and beachies can't afford the medicines from the drug store."

"Is there a lot of illness with those folks?" I was beginning to feel stupid.

"There's a lot of colds, injuries and the aging population has its problems. She's not trying to take the place of a doctor, but her medicine is trusted by the locals."

"I see." But really, I was trying to square Tabitha Blue Smoke with her daughter, Janet. Janet seemed to shun any kind of attention and her mom was doing a *Foghorn* column to add to her reputation.

"I don't want you to mention this to anyone, especially not your secret club, but Tabitha has received a couple of threats about her column at *The Foghorn* office."

Money stolen. Shack burned. A healer gets threats for a newspaper column about herbal cures.

"Curiouser and curiouser, Mom" I yawned. "I have to do my homework and go to bed." I kissed her goodnight and went off to my room, not at all sleepy. I needed to get to Wingnut. I didn't believe his story about breaking into our house to get homework. He was just not that dedicated to the pursuit of knowledge and the honor role.

Sleep was not going to come tonight. I must be reaching adulthood early. Why? Because I've never been this depressed. And I think only adults get this depressed. At least, that's how they look.

The charred remains of our beloved shack sickened me. We could rebuild, but that wasn't the point! Who did it? This new feeling of not being safe on Fred was making me jumpy.

That's it! I needed to get a meeting going. *Let's see what the Buccaneers come up with. Yeah – the plan – we need to get it on.*

CHAPTER EIGHT

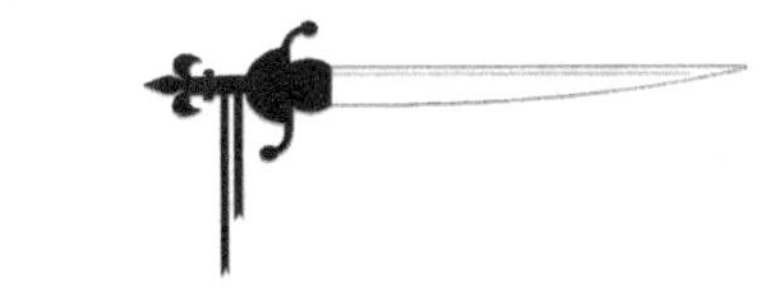

CONNECTING THE DOTS

I woke up to a rare sunny day on Fred. And, tomorrow is Saturday! The plan had been gelling in my mind as I fell asleep. We had to find a new place to meet. Seeing a bunch of us at the burned-out shack would only look odd, and at this point, I didn't know who the enemy was.

Talk spreads like wildfire on Fred. Whoops, no more fires please.

I was pulling on my knee sox when the phone rang, jangling my already jangled nerves. I slipped on my saddle shoes and stood at the top of the stairs trying to hear Mom with no success.

"It's for you, Lily. It's Wingnut!"

What! She knows his code name.

I clunked down the bare wooden steps to the little phone table.

"Yup. What's up?"

"Look under your schoolbooks." The line went dead.

Mom stared.

"Okay, bye." I hung up.

"And what was that all about?" Her arms were folded, and her toe tapped audibly on the kitchen tiles.

"Uh, Frank (I used his real name, giving her a pointed look) called to tell me he had my math homework. Doesn't matter. I redid it." I hated lying to Mom, but I soothed my conscience by telling myself it was for her own good.

She didn't look convinced. I ran back up the stairs and looked under my books. A scrap of paper with a crude drawing of a grinning skull said JON BUCCLEIGH'S CAVE.

"Wingnut, you are a genius!" I whispered.

Of course, an island like Fred would have to have a cave, a dungeon, a huge ancient underground storage place, found only by a few anointed island folks. I needed to talk to Tabatha Blue Smoke. If Mom trusted her, I guess I could.

But we, the Buccaneers knew about the cave. Almost everyone did. It was said to be haunted and that if you went too far into it, you'd never come out. Few Fredites chose to chance those horrors by going in.

The Buccaneers, however, use it when needed. Our meetings in the cave were short, due to the jumpy nerves suffered by all our members.

Now, I needed to get to all of them. I wasn't going to wait until Saturday. I had *the* plan. Are you surprised?

It was October, Science Fair month. The kids who had projects going had a half hour during study hall to contact each other and sort out the details of their projects.

The trouble was, not every Buccaneer was in study hall. But, just maybe, that's okay. Whispering together with half the student body listening in was a recipe for leaks. Forget the study hall.

So, I went to Sister Priscilla, our science teacher, stating my problem that I needed to talk to my science project partners. I convinced her to give me the special pass that allows the bearer to roam the building pretty much at will.

Just an important aside here, Sr. Priscilla's namesake, Saint Priscilla, is the patron saint of nuclear disasters. It's important to have a saint to cover all the bases of possible disasters.

Getting back to the pass. It was a twenty-pound dumb bell from the gym, another example of Sister Superior's sense of humor. The pass was handcuffed to your wrist so you couldn't leave it in some convenient secluded hallway while wreaking havoc all over the building. I wondered why she had such a low opinion of her student body's sense of honor.

First on my list, Ryan, code name Bletchly, or Bletch. He was a ham radio operator. Learned it from his dad who worked at a naval base on Main. We named him after the mansion in England where the code breakers cracked the Nazi code that helped us win WWII. He never took his headphones off. Where he blew an all-out fit, turning a dark shade of blue, was when Father Felix, our chaplain, took them away at Mass one morning. He got them back from the priest who made him promise to start breathing again. When things got tense during a math test, Bletch could be heard tapping Morse code on his desk. Sister Olga, the math teacher, was sure he was sending test question answers to the class who knew the code. Not a bad idea! Maybe we should learn Morse code.

I got the message to everyone by using a simple code, EVAC from CUB. If you hold it up to a mirror, you could figure it out.

Leon, code name Snap Shackle, or Snap, our math genius, chuckled and gave me the thumbs-up.

Amelia, code name Ratchet, was in charge of electronic surveillance. That meant she had a Brownie camera and hid behind trees as she took pictures of suspicious activities. We had to convince her that she could not use pictures she had of kids wearing their knee sox pulled over their saddle shoes as blackmail.

One of the strange phenomena in a school where uniforms were treated as a sign of your faith in God, country and your school, was that any attempt to individualize your appearance via the uniform was deemed a breach of loyalty. We did our best to individualize the uniform. The beanie underwent many forms of origami and even Sister JoAnn was seen to have covered her mouth lest someone should see her giggling at this show of imagination.

So, me/Sprocket, Frank/Wing Nut, Ryan/Bletch, Leon/Snap, and Amelia/Ratchet would all meet at EVAC from CUB, 10AM on Saturday. Bring your tools of the trade and remember our special vow.

We had made it inside. The cave was just a high-ceilinged chamber about twenty by forty feet.

Bletch and Snap were a well-oiled team. Bletch's voice had already changed and his deep baritone bounced off the cave walls. "There's another room, you know."

"What!" came a chorus from the rest of us, sounding hollow with a faint echo as is common in caves.

CHAPTER NINE

EVAC

Walking through the woods to the cave was spooky. The pines and ferns enshrouded with the ever-present fog swirling around them gave a movie set feel for one of the grimmer Grimm's Fairy Tales. Wingnut was snorting as he related the story he had promised to tell me during last week's fire drill.

"My dad told me that when he was in school after WWII, they had air raid drills. And they couldn't talk, or laugh, or breathe almost."

"Sounds familiar," I mumbled tripping over a rotten log.

"The all clear sound was a gong, you know, GOOOOONG! My father was sorta the class clown and he couldn't help himself, and he whispered to his friend, 'That was the sound of the bomb hitting the Empire State Building.' They started to laugh and couldn't stop and got into big trouble. Lots of detention."

To pay tribute to his dad Wing started to laugh uncontrollably, stopping when a branch slapped him in the face.

The cave loomed ahead. Flashlights in hand we entered. Five beams bounced around the far walls of the chamber.

"Stop pushing me, you oaf!" Ratchet shoved her elbow into Wingnut's middle. She pushed her glasses up her nose, arranged her braids, and continued to pick her way around the boulders at the entrance to the cave.

I spotted Wing bringing his arm back, ready to deliver a power-house punch to any part of Ratchet he could land on. I tripped on a stone, but reached him just in time, grabbing his arm. Wing and Ratchet were not the best match among the Buccaneers.

"Stop," I hissed. "Can't you two stow it for a half hour?"

"Stow it?" chuckled Wing. "Spirit of Jon Buccleigh taken' you over?"

"Shut up! You are an oaf."

We had made it inside. The cave was just a high-ceilinged chamber about twenty by forty feet.

Bletch and Snap were a well-oiled team. Bletch's voice had already changed and his deep baritone bounced off the cave walls. "There's another room, you know."

"What!" came a chorus from the rest of us, sounding hollow with a faint echo as is common in caves.

"Yeah. Snap and me found it one day when we were exploring."

"Where?"

Snap pointed and Bletch headed for a solid wall. We all stared, craning our necks to see an opening in the wall of the cave.

Bletch knelt and disappeared.

"Ohhh," chorused the group.

Ratchet screamed, "He's disappeared. I knew this stupid cave was haunted. Now, you've done it," she flung at Snap.

"Your precious boyfriend is just in the next chamber."

Hmm, boyfriend. Whaddya know. I wonder if Bletch knows.

As if by signal, Bletch calmed everyone's fears, yelling up to the group. "C'mon and take a look."

"Hmph," red-faced in the beam of my flashlight, Ratchet looked down the hole by the back wall of the cave.

We had never explored the back of the cave. We didn't come here often, because we used our club house on the beach. It was a bit of a hike through the woods to get here.

The floor of the cave did begin to dip toward the back wall about seven feet from that wall. Partially hidden behind a small scattering of rocks was an opening. Circling it, we aimed our flashlights into the hole, blinding Bletch who uttered a muffled "jerks," and possibly a few other words Father Felix told us would be a direct ticket to hell. The drop into that chamber was about six feet.

"C'mon down," Bletch invited.

One by one we descended into the next chamber.

"Do you think this is where Jon Buccleigh hid his loot?" Wing asked.

"Is this the only other chamber?" I asked.

"We don't know," said Snap. "We just didn't look past here. Seemed dangerous to do without anyone knowing we were in the cave."

"Good thinking," I agreed. "Okay, let's get down to business.

"The oath, please."

We formed a circle, holding hands. This was a crazy stretch for this group. Snap, Bletch and Wing really didn't want to hold hands, at least not with each other. In fact, it usually took a few minutes of slapping each other to get order.

Heads bent, we repeated, "No lies, only facts, good deeds, best friends." The words echoed slightly, leaving a trace of a ringing in my ears. Breaking hand holds we all gave a single clap and found a spot to sit on the floor.

"The meeting has come to order. What do we know and what are we going to do?" As club president, I called on each member. "Wing."

"I didn't tell you, but . . ."

"Oh brother. Wing. What?"

"I went to the clubhouse last night. I snuck out. My parents are really sound sleepers."

"You do that a lot, don't you," Ratchet sniffed.

"How else are you gonna find stuff out?"

Before Ratchet could say another thing, I said, "What did you see there?" in my most patient voice.

"There was somebody shuffling and rooting around in the ashes. I was afraid. So, I buried myself in the sand and watched. He, I think it was a he, left with a box."

"A box? We didn't have any boxes in there. Right?" I looked around at the other four. "Are you sure?" The others shook their heads.

"Nope."

"No."

"Don't remember any boxes."

I looked at Wing. "Anything else?"

"No," said Wing after a brief hesitation.

"Next, Ratchet?"

"You know I take pictures with my Brownie camera?"

Everyone groaned. Ratchet was the class photographer.

"Well, I like to go down to the ferry dock after school when the Five O'clock comes in. I take pictures of the Fredites. I'm thinking of asking your Mom, Sprocket, if I could have a weekly column in *The Foghorn*. I'd take their pictures and interview them."

"Get to the point, Ratch."

"Yeah. It's that there are strangers sometimes. Seems funny that strangers come at five. They don't go anywhere. They hang out at the dock, looking at their watches and then get back on the Alert, and go back to Main or wherever they go.

I've taken their pictures, and I will tell you they are scary looking. So, I don't let them see that I am snapping them."

"Great! Can you get us those snapshots?"

"Of course. You know I develop the film myself."

"Yeah We know," said Wing a bit snidely.

"Shut up. This is important evidence," she shot back.

Boy. I hope Wing and Ratchet never get married.

"She's right, Wing."

I moved on to Bletch and Snap.

"Me and Snap have a theory."

"Let's hear it," we said in unison. Bletch and Snap were the class geniuses, so I was hoping for something profound.

"We've been watching the kids in our class to see if anybody's behavior has changed since the money was stolen."

Snap picked up the story. "Besides our own weird behavior, I noticed that attendance has dropped off for two kids. Our own Wingnut, and Janet Blue Smoke. We know that Wing is just a stupid chronic truant, but we think Janet's absences are mysterious, because her mother is the school nurse. So, we think Janet may know something. What, we don't know."

"Hmm. Yeah, that is strange." I couldn't tell them about the threatening letter her mother received, and I hoped to find out more when I got home.

"We have enough to go on here. Let's take these leads, split up and gather more info. Ratchet, continue what you are doing. Wing, since you are successful at sneakin' out at night, continue your surveillance of the beach hut. Your parents are going to kill me."

"Snap and Blech. You two and me. We're going to split up the school, students and faculty. Yeah, the nuns and Father Felix. And we are going to watch them. Somebody knows something."

The group did a short drum beat on the floor, sounding loud and a little ominous in the cave.

"Before we go, be careful. Look at what we have here. A thief. Strange men on the ferry dock. And, somebody's scared enough to burn down our clubhouse.

I'm scared too, but if we keep our eyes and ears open and stay together, we'll solve this. No fighting." I looked at Wing and Ratchet.

"We'll figure this out. Promise me you'll be careful."

The group murmured their assent. We got up, brushing the dust from our clothes and left the cave.

****

Hovering behind a boulder in the newly discovered chamber, Janet Blue Smoke had heard the whole conversation. But what could she do about it?

Should I tell them what I know? Should I tell Mom? I'm trying to protect her. If I tell, I'll be in real trouble. I can't. I have to solve this myself. Janet thought.

CHAPTER TEN

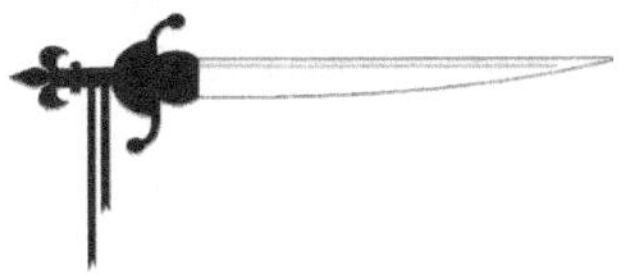

BECCA CIRCLES THE WAGONS

The radio in the kitchen blared out Frank Sinatra singing "Time after Time" as Becca Dawes clicked the flint starter several times before the gas caught on the kitchen stove. She pressed down her annoyance at it.

It's better than that old coal stove.

The gas stove was the first luxury she and husband, Brett, had invested in before he died. They'd meant to modernize the kitchen little by little, but now, with nothing but his small social security check and the very small profit from *The Foghorn*, there was no chance for that shiny new kitchen.

Most of the rehab on the beach shack went into making it a cottage with running water, heat, and electricity, plus a live-in attic.

Becca filled the tea kettle, grateful for the indoor plumbing, and put it on the burner. Rummaging in the old china cabinet she found four cups and saucers that weren't chipped and placed them on the table next to the date nut bread she had just baked.

She loved her china cabinet, table and four chairs. Brett found them in the trash at the ferry dock on Main. With the help of Sibby he brought them home, repaired the broken parts, and gave them to Becca for Christmas their first year on Fred. Becca, over a period of months, had sanded and refinished them. By some miracle, the glass in the doors was not broken out or cracked.

When Brett was fixing the drawers at the cabinet's base, he discovered several bolts of cloth. Cheerful checked ginghams and colorful floral patterns became the curtains in their home as well as napkins and pillow covers. Becca came to Fred with a sewing machine, a gift from her grandmother.

Becca looked around making sure the floor was clean, that Fish and Boots hadn't left any unpleasant tokens on the floor or chairs. The kettle whistled and she added loose tea, wrapping the teapot in a thick towel to keep it warm. Sugar and milk, spoons and forks, plates and those gingham napkins finished her little tea party.

Just in time. A tap sounded at the kitchen door. It was Tabitha Blue Smoke followed by Sibby who took the two steps in a single bound. Tabitha looked nervous, clutching a large leather messenger bag with beautiful Native American beading on the shoulder strap. She wore her navy-blue nurses' uniform, but no cap and nurse shoes. Her jet-black hair was braided, and the braid had feathers and beading twisted in it. She wore moccasins much like the ones I had seen Janet wearing. The fact that she was tall and strong boned made for a woman who would be respected. I thought about the threat she had received and couldn't see her backing down.

Sibby beamed at both ladies, rubbing his hands over the steam from the teapot.

"Mornin', Ladies. Chilly today. Where's the Lass?"

Tabitha gave him a quizzical look while Becca pressed her lips together, seeming to hide a grin.

"Lily!" Becca called from the foot of the stairs. "C'mon star witness. Time to spill the beans."

CHAPTER ELEVEN

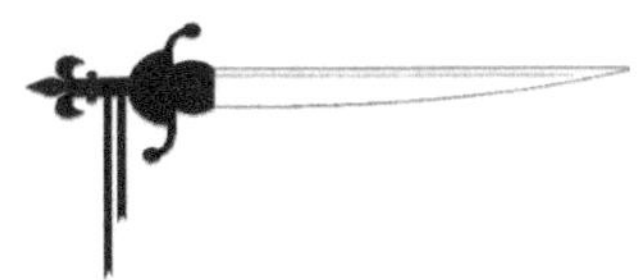

A CLOUD OF BLUE SMOKE

"Lily!" Becca repeated from the foot of the stairs. "C'mon star witness. Time to spill the beans."

I came down the stairs, sniffing at the aroma coming from the kitchen. "Oh yum. I'm starving."

"Me too," declared Sibby.

"Well?" Mom looked at me. "You called this meeting," she accused, forcing a stiff grin over her worried face. She poured the tea and invited everyone to sit down.

"Okay," I said. "Mom, Sibby, Mrs. Blue Smoke. This is what we've got. The money me and my classmates raised to buy toys for city kids was stolen, our clubhouse was torched, and Mrs. Blue Smoke got a threatening letter. I think these events are not the usual thing on Fred. What do you think?"

Mom had served the date nut bread while I recited that list, and the four of us chewed and stirred, ate and drank, always a good way to give everybody time to think. I didn't need time to think. Between what I had said and what I had held back from the meeting in the cave, I was convinced all these things were related. What we needed was why and how and who. We had the where and when.

With a slight tremor Mrs. Blue Smoke put her teacup in the saucer causing a telltale rattle. She reached into her messenger bag, and looking at me said, "Lily, why don't you read this?"

I reached for the single sheet of paper she offered, wanting to reach out and steady her shaking hand. "Thanks, Mrs. Blue Smoke."

"Oh, just call me Blue Smoke. That's my true name. Or just Blue."

"Sure, cool, ah, neat. Thanks, I mean."

I unfolded the note, read it, and dropped it on the table as if it were on fire.

"Dam . . . arn. Fingerprints! Who touched this, Mrs. . . Blue Smoke?"

"Just me, Lily."

"Mom. Do you have tweezers?"

Sibby gave me an admiring look. "Good thinking, Lass."

I caught Mom's grin as she turned to pour more tea. She rummaged in the junk drawer and pulled out a pair of needle- nosed plyers that was stuck to a roll of tape and a bunch of rubber bands. She pried them loose and handed them to me.

I picked up the note and held it to the light coming in from the kitchen window. There were two grease spots and a brown smudge.

"Blue Smoke, were these here when you got the note?"

I'll look at these later with my magnifier.

"Yup. They were."

I cleared my throat and read.

Where does Janet play, Tabitha?

What is in those medicines you give out?

Is your bedroom window locked at night?

Is Rebecca Dawes a good friend or just your Foghorn boss?

Does Janet like Lily Dawes?

My stomach fell a little further with each question. Every one of them was a threat against Blue Smoke, her daughter, and even me and Mom.

Sibby got up and paced around the kitchen, slapping a fist into his palm. "We have to take measures to protect you ladies and girls," he declared with a final punch to the door jamb. "I have folks in the beach shacks who can help." He sucked on the knuckles he had just smacked into the door jamb.

"This is serious." I let the note fall to the table. I looked at Mom and Sibby and Blue Smoke. The three serious faces confirmed what I already knew.

CHAPTER TWELVE

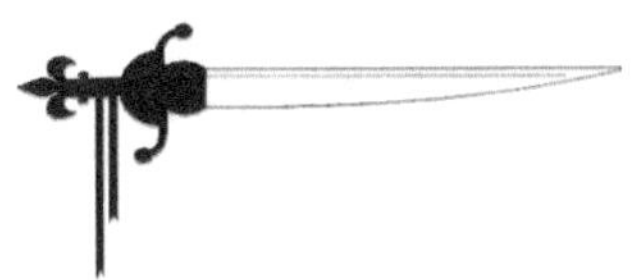

NATIVE AMERICAN MEDICINE

"Are you friends with Janet Blue Smoke?" Mom asked shaking herself free of the stunning words in the letter.

"Not really. She keeps to herself." I glanced at Blue Smoke, but her eyes were looking at her hands tightly clasped in her lap.

"I'm having trouble with Janet." She admitted looking at Mom and Sibby. "She disappears for hours at a time, and sometimes doesn't come home until the middle of the night."

"Oh, Tabitha." Mom covered Janet's mom's hands with her own. "Have some more tea. You're ice cold."

Blue Smoke looked at Sibby and then me. "Do either of you ever see her around?"

"Nope. I'm sorry," I said. Sibby just shook his head, frowning at some distant vision.

This is really scary. I better talk this over with the Buccaneers. I made a mental note.

"I'll ask my friends."

"And I'll ask the Beachies," added Sibby.

"I have something to report." I cleared my throat clutching my teacup for warmth but finding it had gone cold.

I looked from face to face. "One of my buddies was telling us when we had a meeting about our clubhouse that she's noticed some strangers getting off the five o'clock ferry. Just hanging out for a while and then getting back on."

"Another thing to watch," muttered Sibby. He perked up, looking at Blue Smoke. "The threats are against you and your daughter, Becca and Lily. The common thread is your medicine and *The Foghorn*. They attack your medicines and then they attack *The Foghorn*, which is your market, in a way."

"Maybe if you tell us about your practice, we can figure out what the connection is," I piped up.

"Exactly my thoughts, Lass!"

Arf, I thought, but kept it to myself. My mind was racing a mile a minute, wanting to talk to the Buccaneers to get this all figured out.

Mom said, "Well, Tabitha is the school nurse. She is licensed. We all know that. We also know she writes a column for *The Foghorn* where she shares Native American healing arts. That's the connection among the four of us. The girls are a way of threatening Tab and me. The key seems to be the promotion of her healing arts. Why is that a threat?"

Spot on, Mom! I thought, and that's what I'll take to the next meeting.

"Maybe it's something in the cures you're promotin'," said Sibby.

"Maybe one of the tribe members died from them or think they did. There's no doctor on Fred for you to compete with," Mom added.

"Do you get any complaints? Are some folks in the tribes against your cures?" Sibby asked.

"Yes. I get some who slam the door in my face. They think it's the money. And I don't get it, because what I charge for my treatments is a fraction of what the pharmacy charges."

"What's in your cures, Mrs . . .. ah . . . Blue Smoke?"

"Herbs, mostly in the form of teas. Some in cough drop form. Salves you rub on your skin. I make them all myself. My mother was a healer too. She was lucky enough to go to school, and she wrote down everything she learned from her mother and other tribal healers.

The most popular are the teas for digestion, and the willow bark for headaches. Some of the older folks like the salve for sore joints. This island has many of the plants I need to make those. I go to Main and then to the mainland for the other materials I need.”

“So, in a way, you are competing with modern medicine. If there was a pharmacy here on Fred or a doctor who got his supplies from a drug company, there would be a conflict,” Mom said.

“Maybe. But I don’t deal with serious or complicated problems like diabetes or strokes or heart attacks, or, God forbid, cancer,” Blue Smoke frowned thinking this over.

“There’s got to be a link though,” Sibby said, scratching his chin where a beard stubble was beginning to sprout.

“I have an idea,” I said. Why not, in your next column, give one of your cures that there is an easy modern medicine for, like penicillin for a bad skin infection from a cut. What's your cure? See if you get another letter."

"Or worse," said Sibby.

The adults started fussing with the dishes and stuff, and when no one was looking, I snatched the note to examine it further.

I hope Blue Smoke doesn't miss it or doesn't care if I take it.

I headed out the door to find the Buccaneers before anybody could ask me where I was going or delivered a warning I wasn't going to pay attention to anyway.

CHAPTER THIRTEEN

A CALL TO ARMS

Breaking free from the house and the pondering adults, I ran down the beach under the cover of fog. I headed for the clubhouse ruins where I might find Wing.

"Where could he be?"

The burned-out hulk came in and out of focus as wisps of fog drifted in the light offshore breeze.

"Oh, thank God!" I huffed as the fog lifted a bit and revealed Wing talking to one of the Beachies. "What's up?" I gasped bending with my hands on my knees trying to catch my breath. Little stars danced across my vision.

"What's up yourself," Wing said, bending to look at my face.

I pulled Tabitha Blue Smoke's threatening note out of my pocket. "Just read this." My breathing eased, and I watched Wing's face as he read.

"You okay?" Sunny, one of the new Beachies patted my back. He seemed young next to Sibby. He had an army fatigue jacket with the symbol for the Big Red One on it. It was famous for the bravery they showed the world in the war that just passed. One arm of the jacket was pinned to the body of the jacket. It was missing that arm.

"Yeah. I'm okay. How about you?" I asked to be polite.

"Yeah. Yeah. But there's a lotta stuff goin' on here." He gestured to the charred timbers.

"Like what? Did you see who did it?" *Maybe I'd get lucky.*"

"I came here last night with a flashlight. There were no footprints here. He pointed to an area that would have been the floor of our clubhouse.

"I squat in that hut next door," Sunny said. "Ya know, I don't sleep nights. Too many bad dreams."

What we knew about Sunny was that he served in the war at the Battle of the Bulge, one of the most ferocious battles of WWII. That's where he lost his arm. Sibby told my mom that he was the only survivor in his company. I overheard that conversation because as a Buccaneer, I pledge to eavesdrop, snoop, and generally gather information about life and times on Fred.

"Tell her, Sunny," Wing urged.

"Yeah. I was getting' there." He pushed his hair, which was very black and surprisingly shiny, out of his eyes and squinted at the ocean for a second or two. Then he told me what he saw.

"There was a girl. At least, I thought it was a girl. She knelt right there." He pointed and you could see the depression in the sand.

"That's it?"

"No, I saw her like sifting through the sand. She did that for about an hour. Then she stood up and pushed the sand back in place with her feet."

"I guess she wanted to cover her footprints," Wing said.

"Who was she?"

"I don't know," Sunny said." It was dark. It coulda been you!" He looked at me. "About the same size, and definitely a girl. Ya know, she had that body type." He blushed a bit.

"This just keeps getting weirder and weirder," Wing said, shaking his head. "Oh." He roused himself. "Wait till I tell you what I found." I wasn't sure if he was scared or proud that he had a secret to tell.

"So?"

"I went into the cave late yesterday."

"What! Alone? Are you nuts?"

"Probably." He shrugged, grinning. "Isn't that why you call me Wingnut?"

"Okay. Give. Obviously, you found something," I said.

"I went into the other chamber with my flashlight and really took a good look. There are two other passages leading off that room. They're real hard to see because there are overhangs in front of the tunnels."

"Tunnels? How did you find them?"

"I dropped my flashlight, and it went out. Scared the crap outta me. I crawled around on the ground to find the flashlight because it rolled away. Then, in the darkness, I noticed a dim light coming from somewhere. Since I was on the ground, I could see under the overhangs and I saw the tunnels. There was a breeze and I could smell the bay."

"What did you do?"

"I was spooked. I grabbed my light and got outta there."

"We have to go back and explore," I said.

Sunny looked at me and shook his head. "You guys gotta stop doin' this stuff without tellin' anybody."

"We will tell someone this time." I sort of lied. We do always leave one Buccaneer behind just in case we don't come back from one of these explorations.

"We've done this before. We had to find and rescue my neighbor's dog. He got wedged between some rocks at the tide line. We had to get the dog out before the tide started coming in, or he'd drown. And if we got stuck there, it wouldn't be just the dog who was in deep trouble."

We have to go back. Too late today We have school tomorrow, I thought.

"Sprocket. Wake up." Wing shook me out of my daydream.

"I didn't tell you the good part. There was stuff on the floor of the second chamber. And I think I know whose it was."

"Don't tell me now!"

"Don't worry," Wing said with that cat ate the canary look. "I'm saving it for the meeting, and my surprise is in the cave anyway."

"Holy cow! We need another meeting. After school tomorrow."

"Can I help," Sunny offered. "I don't like the sound of this."

"Yes, Sunny. Don't tell anyone, okay. Just give us a day to check this out."

"You got it. But just one day. That's 5:30pm or 17:30 military time tomorrow."

We headed back to our own homes. I jumped at every flitting shadow that peeked out of the fog banks.

At home, I took out Blue Smoke's note, got out my fingerprint dust and magnifying glass. Where, you ask, did I get this dust. Easy. Charcoal from the fireplace. I made it.

First, I looked at the stains with my magnifier. Grease spots and maybe ketchup, but the red stuff could be blood. Then I gently sifted the charcoal dust over the note, and then just as gently, blew it off. There was only one set of prints and a smudge which I probably made. The prints were easily identified to one person because of an unusual scar on the thumb. I'd have to ask to see Blue Smoke's thumb.

My conclusion. The person who wrote the note was a sloppy eater but wore gloves. My findings didn't matter, because I'd have to give the note back to Blue Smoke. Unless she wanted to contact the police, the note seemed to lack good clues.

CHAPTER FOURTEEN

SQUEAKING THROUGH
IN MORE WAYS THAN ONE

"Thanks, Mom. I held up my lunch bag and gave her a thumbs up.

She smiled.

"What are you going to do today, Mom?" I was worried about her being at *The Foghorn* by herself.

"I need to get this week's paper out, Lily. Blue Smoke has a new column, and I wrote a story about the fires."

"Don't forget my story about the stolen money."

"No, I won't."

"Lock the doors, Mom. While you're there alone."

"Yes, I will, but Sibby said he'd drop by to help with the press, so I won't be alone."

"Ohhhh, Siiiby," I trilled.

Mom blushed and I left, letting the screen door slam shut. I giggled. Every time I did this, Boots staggered out of his bed, wuffing for about ten seconds, and Fish howled, strutting about looking like someone had electrocuted her.

"Lily!" Mom demanded, hoping I'd soon stop this dumb trick on our pets.

"Bye, Mom."

Hah, so Sibby's stopping by. I wondered about that gleam I saw in his eye. Good. Somebody cares about Mom, and I can't keep an eye on her when I'm in school.

Homeroom looked normal. It was the first normal thing for me since the fire. Prayers were said. Pledge of Allegiance and announcements followed.

"Lily Dawes, please report to the nurse's office immediately", boomed the intercom. This was not the voice of the student who usually made the announcements. It was Sister Superior. My stomach flipped over, and my hands went ice cold.

I gathered my books, fumbling and red faced. The entire homeroom stared at me.

"Don't worry," I tossed back at them. "They heard I found a cure for the common cold."

The nurse's office was warm, unlike most of the classrooms. It was cheerful with lots of plants and a bright blue curtain hiding the two beds reserved for headaches, cramps and feverish students waiting for their ride home. It smelled like alcohol, but there was a hint of ginger and peppermint. Hmm. Blue Smoke's herbal teas?

"Good morning, Mrs. Blue Smoke," I said, heart pounding.

"Lily, any minute Sister Superior will be here. Do you have the threatening letter? I want it back."

I fished in my book bag, retrieving it, and handed it over. "Sorry, I wasn't thinking." I lied. I never stop thinking.

A second later Sr. Superior glided into the room under an aura of starch and ivory soap, keys and rosaries jingling to complete her officious image.

"Good morning, Sister." I dipped a brief curtsy hoping she would be impressed with my courtesy.

Behind her, Father Felix strode in, nodding to the two ladies, his gaze coming to rest on me.

Oh boy. I gulped, starting an emergency Hail Mary.

Father Felix started with, "Lily, this is really important."

"Have you seen Janet?" Blue Smoke pleaded, her voice catching on Janet's name.

I felt my eyes widening to what I bet was my hair line. I just stared and shook my head. "No, Ma'am."

"Are you sure, Lily? This isn't some stunt you and your buddies are playing, is it?"

"I haven't seen Janet. She mostly keeps to herself. Not because we don't try to include her, Father. She's a loner."

I was beginning to feel angry.

What did he mean, by stunts, and my buddies? Did he know about the Buccaneers?"

I stammered. "Do you think that me and my buddies shouldn't be trying to find the money we raised for those city kids?"

Cool it, Lily. I said to myself, but boy did he hit a sore spot.

"I'm sorry, Lily, but you are a natural leader, and it seems there's always something going on, sort of an undercurrent." He looked at me, head cocked, with a quizzical expression.

"Father, we came to you for help when the money went missing. You wanted us to offer it up as some sort of sacrifice. We couldn't accept that. We would like your help, but we'll continue to try to solve this mystery without it."

"Lily!" Sister Superior, who'd turned purple, exclaimed.

"It's okay, Miriam . . .er . . . Sister Miriam. She has a point. These kids put a lot of work into that fund raiser. We should be proud of them."

Shock waves washed over me.

An admission of error!

But even more stunning, this was a true gem. Sister Superior's name was Miriam. I was getting drunk on the power of possessing this information. The only other thing I needed to find out was if she had hair under that bonnet.

"I need to find Janet." Blue Smoke cleared her throat and tapped loudly on her desk, bringing us back to reality.

"Do you have a picture of Janet? We could show it to the Beachies to see if they've seen her. One of my friends told me she sometimes sees her at the ferry dock. You could ask around there.”

“Good idea, Lily. I knew you’d have something,” Father said.

“If she’s not found by tonight, I’m calling the tribal police,” Blue Smoke said, face set in stone.

I went back to class and as the day progressed, the message to meet at the cave right after dismissal was passed to all the Buccaneers. This was too serious to lay low and play possum.

“Where’s Ratchet?” I asked as Wing, Bletch and Snap, and of course, me, trudged to the cave.

Wing filled me in saying, “She said she was going to the ferry dock to take pictures so that we can identify the strangers and she will also keep an eye out for Janet.”

“Good thinking,” I grunted as we climbed to the entrance of the cave.

“Okay. First, what did you see on the cave floor?”

We dropped into the second room where we found a bunch of food wrappers and some old homework sheets. They were from our math class, but no name. "We'll have to do handwriting analysis."

"Ever the crime scene detective," Wing muttered sarcastically.

We had some paper bags with us. We labeled each, packaging the various items from the floor.

"Let's check out those tunnels, Bucc's."

Just as Wing ducked to show us one of the tunnels, a low moan barely vibrated in the cave. Everyone froze.

"Shhh," hissed Snap.

Again, the moan came, only louder, interrupted by some short clicks.

"Let's get out of here!" Snap and Bletch scrambled toward the entrance, me and Wing in hot pursuit.

Ratchet didn't want to stand out like a sore thumb. Surveillance required melting into the scenery. The outfit channeled Rosie the Riveter. Rosie, as you may have heard, was another heroine in American history.

CHAPTER FIFTEEN

MEANWHILE, AT THE FERRY DOCK

Ratchet would much rather be called by her real name, Amelia. Especially since one of her heroines was Amelia Erhardt, the aviatrix who made news-worthy flights around the world. She disappeared somewhere in the Pacific, never to be found. Ratchet just couldn't resist the mystery of it all.

However, she would be true to her oath as a Buccaneer and fulfill her mission. She struggled with how to accomplish this. Most days she went to the ferry dock dressed in her reporter's costume consisting of a many-pocketed jacket, borrowed men's trousers, a cap with a green visor, and several cameras strung around her neck, most of which did not work.

But her trusty Brownie never failed her. Notepad in hand she snapped photos of the ferry passengers going to and from Main. She was too shy, at this point, to go up to them and get that "scoop".

Today was different. She didn't want to stand out like a sore thumb. Surveillance required melting into the scenery. The outfit for this assignment had her pigtails tucked into a red bandana, her thick lensed glasses hidden behind her dad's aviator shades, and a dark blue jumpsuit, two sizes too big, borrowed from her brother who worked at Fred's only gas station. She was channeling Rosie the Riveter. Rosie, as you may have heard, was another heroine in American history. She and her millions of sisters made the planes, tanks and ships that won the recent World War. Since the war effort for Rosie was over for now, Amelia still stuck out like a sore thumb.

"Hey, Sis. Halloween's over," called out one of the day trippers.

Embarrassed, she hid the bandana and pulled out her braids. She kept the glasses, and the coveralls were a must, since taking them off meant she would be walking around in her undies.

Her Brownie was in her pocket. There were several huge hemlocks near the ticket office. Amelia hid among them and started snapping. She got a shot of everyone, thinking she needed to make a file of all the regulars, so that any strangers would stand out.

It was getting pretty boring. What was she thinking? This is a lame idea, but duty called, and she settled herself more comfortably. The scents of tar, salt water, and creosoted wood planking joined the piney aroma of the hemlocks to provide a perfume Amelia came to call home.

Fiddling with the camera, she almost missed her. Amelia looked up just in time. Janet trotted down the path to the ferry dock. She could have missed her because she had a jacket with a hood. But Janet always wore beaded moccasins and her pigtails had feathers instead of bows. One braid escaped the hood sealing her identity for Amelia.

Amelia, now in Ratchet mode, started snapping again. Janet turned her way and Ratchet's heart almost stopped. Ratchet knew how important it was to identify Janet as Janet in her series of photos. Taking a breath and holding it, she snapped away.

When Ratchet returned to check out the folks getting off the ferry, the strangers she had seen on other days came down the gangplank. Snap! Snap! Snap! They surrounded Janet, one grabbing her arm, the other talking to her, right in her face, grim and threatening. Janet pulled her arm away and snapped back at the stranger who had confronted her.

The other man jammed something in her pocket. "Just do it," he growled. This was an easy lip read for Ratchet, a skill necessary for a well-trained snoop, er, journalist. Janet turned and ran back up the path. The men got back on the boat.

Ratchet took out her notepad and described each.

Number One - tall, thin, suspect him to be bald (no hair sticking out of his hood, tan hiking boots, missing thumb on left hand.

Number Two – also tall, bushy hair, glasses.

Number Three – The hand grabber. Shorter than the other two, blue eyes, light hair blooming out of a black watch cap. Tattoo on right hand, impossible to make out.

Number Four – Short, maybe five foot six, impossible to see details, wearing gloves and a hood. Wonder if it is a woman, or someone we might recognize.

"Hey, Amelia!"

Amelia nearly peed her blue jumpsuit.

"What are you doing in that get-up, hiding in the bushes?"

Amelia gasped, trying to bring her heart rate down. This was Amelia's hero on site, Red Winterberry. She had been a WASP during the war, a Women's Air Service Pilot, testing and flying fighter planes. She was now the captain on the Alert, the ferry that went between Main and Fred.

Red was tiny, no more than five foot and very thin. Her blue eyes were lined from squinting, probably from her years piloting planes and boats. Her signature red hair was rolled up in some sort of up-do with a baseball cap crammed on top.

"Red. I need a favor. It's very important. But you have to keep it a secret. Okay?"

"What is it. You look all shook up."

"Some strangers get off the ferry, meet someone or just mill around, and get back on. They just met one of my classmates and it looked like they were threatening her."

"Yeah. I know who you mean. I wondered about them myself. What do you want me to do? They don't break any laws."

"Just watch them and keep an eye out for Ja . . .my classmate. I'll come back tomorrow with more information."

"Will do, Amelia. But I don't like the sound of this. If I don't like what I see, I'm calling the Marines."

Ratchet left, thinking, *Yeah, maybe a combo of Buccaneers and Marines will figure this out. What the heck is up with Janet?*

CHAPTER SIXTEEN

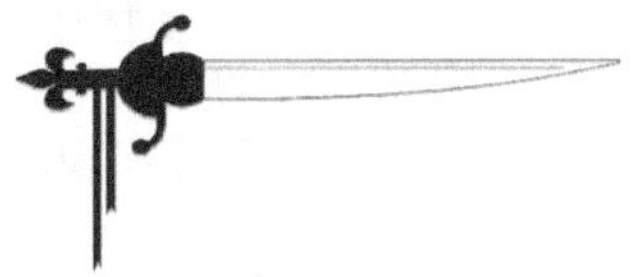

THE SOUND OF THE FOGHORN

"It's 3:30," Sibby said, looking up from the ancient press where he was loading ink. "Wasn't Lily supposed to meet you here? "he added, wiping his hands.

Becca sat at an enormous roll-top desk; its pigeonholes filled with files, its surface showing years of ink stains, and an eighty-seven-year history of information carved or impressed by reporters and editors on the writing surface.

Two smaller desks in the office held typewriters. These old machines worked and were used, but belonged in a museum, which by the way, Becca was working on.

The window bay was filled with potted native ferns, the wide plank pine floors gleamed, and the pot-bellied stove waited to warm the office in a week or two, as Fred got really raw weather by Halloween.

Becca furiously drummed on the ink blotter and stared at the door. *The Foghorn* office occupied the same store front it had when it opened in 1860, a year of terrible news in America; South Caroline seceded from the Union which set the Civil War in motion.

From the outside the office was floor to ceiling, approximately twelve feet, of glass. Etched in the glass and bordered in gold leaf was the masthead of *The Foghorn* with the date. The front door was half glass, half oak. Mom had restored the door which had long since lost its finish.

"Becca, Oh Becca?" Sibby broke into her concentration as she worked on some puzzle known only to her

"What. Oh. Sorry. I'm just trying to put this all together. When did it start? We've never had this kind of trouble on Fred. At least, not since Jon Buccleigh disappeared."

"You remember that, eh?" Sibby teased.

"No, Sibby. But I do read island history. A ghost of a smile played across Becca's face. "Sibby?"

"Yeah. Aye?"

"Thank you for all your help." Becca turned to him, tears in her eyes.

He put down the inky rag and started toward her when the door burst open. Ratchet, red-faced and huffing, gulped, "Where is Spr . . . Lily?"

"Whoa, Lassie. What's the matter?"

"I just saw Janet! At the ferry dock. I need to find Lily"

"You need to sit down and catch your breath," Becca said. "I'm going to call Blue Smoke. She has been worried sick about her."

Becca dialed Blue Smoke just as Lily, Wing, Snap and Bletch trooped into the small Foghorn office.

CHAPTER SEVENTEEN

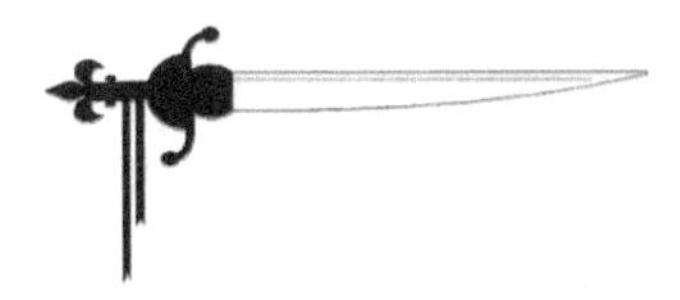

IT'S COMING TOGETHER

We raced from the cave to *The Foghorn*. As we were packaging the "evidence", I saw stuff I think was Janet's. We had to tell Mom and Blue Smoke what we found.

I had such a stitch in my side from running. What a relief as *The Foghorn* office came in sight. Pushing open the door we were surprised to see Ratchet.

Sibby sang, "Hail, hail, the gang's all here. What the heck do we care . . ."

"Shhhh!" Becca commanded, free hand over her ear. She was dialing Blue Smoke's number.

"Yes, Tabitha, we think we found Janet. Can you come to *The Foghorn*?" After a brief pause, Becca placed the phone on its cradle.

"I have . . ." Ratchet started.

"We found ..." I said at the same time.

"One at a time!" Sibby pounded his large fist on the table, grabbing the newly printed page of *The* Foghorn as it fluttered toward the floor.

"Okay, Amelia. You go first. You got here first."

"I have photos right here." She patted the camera. "Of Janet. On the ferry dock. And she is talking with some strange guys who were not exactly friendly to her."

"Can you develop them quickly," asked Sibby.

"Yes, I can. I'll go home right now and do it."

"Do it," everyone said in a chorus of encouragement.

"And I asked my friend, Red Winterberry, you know, the ferry captain, to look out for anything else suspicious."

"Go thinking," I said. "Go!"

Ratchet lunged for the door, clutching her camera with one hand, and straight arming the door with the other. Just in time to straight arm Blue Smoke, almost knocking her down.

"Oh. Sorry. So sorry. Gotta go." And Ratchet was gone.

Blue Smoke recovered, looking around at the crowd, an air of expectation making her seem to vibrate.

"Where's Janet?" she said, disappointment rearranging her features.

"We think we know where Janet's been," I said, pushing my way forward in the now crowded office.

"Tell me." Blue smoke collapsed into a chair.

"Well, we have a theory."

There was a collective groan.

"Oh. Get to the point, Lily," Becca urged, and the crowd mumbled agreement with this sentiment, feeling the growing frustration.

"We have been meeting in Jon Buccleigh's cave since the fire, and we found some stuff on the floor there."

I neglected to talk about the secret room and tunnels just yet, having a hunch that the adults in the room would find these explorations reason to forbid us to use the cave.

You can never be too careful with adults when it comes to these kinds of things.

"Look. We collected them in paper bags."

"Ever the detective," Mom muttered.

"Hmm. Great minds think alike," Wing concurred.

"We haven't had time to analyze them get," I said ignoring his sarcasm.

Another group groan.

"No time like the present, Lassie."

"Arf." I looked at Sibby. "Lassie's a dog, Sibby."

"Aye." He smiled and winked.

What? I thought.

I dumped each bag on the table Sibby was sitting on. One was a candy wrapper. Another was a homework sheet. The third was a hair clip.

"Look at the homework sheet, Blue Smoke." She looked at it. There was no name on it, but she said, "This is Janet's. Her math teacher spoke to me at school about the bad grade.

That's her hair clip too. See the bead work. Her grandmother made it for her. And that's a wrapper from her favorite candy bar, Bit-O-Honey."

"That cinches it. Janet was in the cave, but what was she doing there," Mom said.

"Blue Smoke, the girl who bumped into you before has some photos of Janet meeting some strangers from the ferry," I added.

"Oh, God. What is this all about?" She put her head in her hands.

Mom went to her and put her arms around her to give her time to absorb all of this. It also gave me some time to think.

Could Janet have stolen the money? And burned the clubhouse? And who were these strange men? I hope Ratchet doesn't take too long developing the film.

A chair scraped, and Blue Smoke got up. "I'm going to find Janet and take this to the Tribal Council."

As she got up to go, Sibby took her arm. "Wait for Amelia's photos."

"And, here. Take the clues." I thrust the bags at her.

She took them. "Call me when Amelia returns. Right now, I need to find Janet."

She moved quickly to the door only to be struck by it again, as Janet rushed to enter.

CHAPTER EIGHTEEN

THE TROUBLE WITH JANET

"Ouch! Janet! What's going on?" Blue Smoke demanded rubbing her arm

"We were so worried about you," Mom said.

"You'd better explain," Sibby added. "It looks like you're in a bit of trouble."

Nothing like making a body feel welcomed, I thought.

"You look awful," her mother continued, not even giving Janet a moment to catch her breath.

"You're in danger, Mom," Janet said. "And your Buccaneers are too." She looked at me and I felt like she just challenged me to a duel.

"That's all I have to say right now." She folded her arms defiantly and looked out the window.

"You came to warn us," I said. "Of what?"

"I can't tell you. But Mom, you have to stop writing your column."

"What? Why?"

"I can't tell you!"

"Okay. We're going home. And Janet, we will meet with the Tribal leaders. And WILL get to the bottom of this. At least we'll be safe on the reservation."

There was no official reservation. It was a Native American settlement, like a self-contained town with no borders.

Janet was dirty, her uniform shirt had a torn sleeve, and she looked like a cornered wild animal. Blue Stoke took her arm and they left in silence.

I looked at Mom and Sibby. The Buccaneers looked at me. "What do you know, Lily?" Mom said.

"No more than I just told you. I'm as confused as you are."

"Why does Janet think her mother must stop writing her column on health?" Mom asked.

"Who is Janet meeting at the ferry dock," Sibby added.

"And is our stolen money and the fire at our clubhouse related to any of this?"

"It all started with the stolen money," Mom said.

"We didn't think any of the Freds would steal our money, and now we know there are strangers at the ferry dock. Where else have they gone on the island?"

Could those strangers be the connection? I thought.

"I'm guessing the fire was to put you off trying to find out who stole the money, scare you, like," Sibby suggested.

"But it had the opposite effect," I replied.

"And very soon after the fire Blue Smoke got the first threatening letter," Mom added.

"Yeah, Mom. And that letter links you, me, Janet and Blue Smoke."

"So, Blue Smoke gets the threat and now we know what spooked whoever wrote that letter. It's the health column offering Native American cures," Mom concluded. "What is so threatening about those cures? They are probably less dangerous than prescription medicines. Why don't we look at her columns and see if there's a thread that will give us a clue?"

I like this plan.

"The first one was a headache cure that I used and worked," said Sibby. "Willow bark tea with a lavender filled pillow over the eyes when you lie down."

"Most folks just take aspirin. You can get that anywhere," I said.

"There's also some pretty strong prescription medications for bad headaches," Mom offered.

"The second one was for sore throat. Also, herbal tea and slippery elm tablets. The one that goes in today is for arthritis joint pain." Sibby noted looking at the page set-up he was about to print for the new edition. "They all seem pretty harmless to me."

He put the page down, rubbing his chin. "I have an idea. I have to go to Main and check something out."

Sibby left, hurrying to catch the five o'clock ferry.

"Sibby," I called. "Look out for the strangers." I got a thumbs-up, and he was gone.

"Let's lock up, Lily. Wing, Ryan and Leo, time to go home."

This waiting is really getting on my nerves. What is taking Ratchet so long? Her snapshots could've maybe helped Sibby.

CHAPTER NINETEEN

TABITHA BLUE SMOKE'S MEDICINE

Janet and her mom got home just in time for a loud knock at the door. It was Timothy Walking Tree.

"Good thing you locked up, Blue," he said, his leathery face showing concern.

"Why, Tim?" Blue clutched at Janet's arm.

What now? she thought.

"I was comin' around to drop your mail, and I see these two guys at your door, not knockin', ya know, but tryin' the knob. I faded back a bit to see what they were up to. They went to the windows and tried 'em, then to the back door. I was about to call in reinforcements when they gave up and left."

"Is there a council meeting tonight, Tim?"

"Yup. And you'd better go. This is no laughing matter!" With this, Tim left.

Blue Smoke took Janet by the shoulders. "You are going to tell me what this is all about. You're thirteen years old. No matter what you may be involved in, the only way out is to fess up and let me help."

"Janet, we've gotten a threatening letter. Someone is trying to break into our house. I'm terrified. I need you to tell me what this is all about."

Janet pulled away.

"Okay, daughter. I will bring this up to the council tonight and let them decide what to do with you. I hope they give you a term in the medicine tent."

"No. Wait."

"Well?"

"I stole the money from the Buccaneers."

Blue Smoke just stared at her daughter, mouth opened, looking like you could blow her over with a sneeze.

"That's not the whole story, Mom. These men came one day about a month ago. They said they were interested in learning about the Native American culture here on Fred. I told them about our tribes, and especially about your 'Indian medicines. They told me to steal the money from the sacristy. Then you got the threatening letter, and they keep coming and giving me stuff for you to sell."

"How did they know any of this? They must have known about my healing business before they spoke with you."

"I asked them just that, Mom," Janet said, wiping tears from her eyes. "They said to do just what I was told, or they'd burn down our house. Mom! Obviously. There can't be two thieves with the same idea."

"Wait. Did they burn the clubhouse?"

"Yeah, to scare me. They said it was to keep me honest. I know, poor choice of words."

"What was this all about? It couldn't be about the money from the fund raiser."

"No. It was to keep me from talking like I'm doing now. They would use it to blackmail me."

"What do they get out of this? I still don't understand."

"They said they wanted you to 'push' prescription drugs to our tribes, along with your herbal cures."

"This is very strange, Janet. Where do they get these drugs, and why here, and why us? What kind of medicines?"

"I don't know. But I think it's illegal for them to be doing this."

"It's illegal for them to blackmail you into committing a crime, and to send me threatening letters. That's it. I will ask for a private meeting with the Council leaders after the public meeting."

"What is all this about, Blue. I've never seen you so rattled."

"I will let you hear it from Janet. I have some ideas of what to do, but I respect you, my elder, and need your wisdom. And Janet needs your understanding."

The Council meeting was always held in a building called a long house, which was a replica of the ones used by the ancestors of the North Breeze Tribe. Janet and Blue Smoke arrived late. Janet seemed defeated, shoulders slumped, looking at her shoes and chewing on her nails. Blue Smoke just looked angry.

Coffee and tea with home-baked goods were always served before the meeting. Blue Smoke caught Tim's eye, indicating she wanted to speak with him. He was one of the tribal elders.

"Janet and I need to meet with the elders privately," she said.

"Is it about the folks I saw at your place today?"

"Yes, but it's about a lot more, and we need the tribes' help and wisdom."

Tim could see the fear and worry on Blue Smoke's face. "Okay. Just as soon as the meeting ends, go to my place and I'll tell the others."

"Thank you, Tim. See you later."

The meeting seemed to drag even more than usual, and when the closing came at 9:00PM Blue jumped out of her seat and pulled Janet out of the long house. Tim's place was just a short distance away, a beautiful log cabin surrounded by the tall pine trees that were the dominant vegetation on Fred.

Tim came up behind them. "The others will be along soon. C'mon in."

The inside of the house was warmed by a huge pot belly stove in the middle of the main room. Tim's wife, Stella, was a weaver, evidenced by the many rugs and wall hangings. Tim's animal carvings were also spotted around the room.

"What is all this about, Blue. I've never seen you so rattled."

"I will let you hear it from Janet. I have some ideas of what to do, but I respect you, my elder, and need your wisdom. And Janet needs your understanding."

Janet revealed the whole story to the elders who looked from Blue to Janet not showing anger or outrage, but also looking very stern.

At the end Tim said, "Janet, why didn't you come directly to us, or to Father Felix?"

"I. . .I," Janet cried, gulping and gasping between sobs.

"Did they hurt you?"

"Noonoo, but they scared me. They threatened Mom. I had to protect her."

"But here you are, telling us now."

"What can I do? Can you protect my mother?"

"First we must give the money back. Do you have it?"

"No. I had to give it to them."

"Do you have to meet with them again?"

"Yes. Tomorrow."

The elders looked at each other, talking over what to do.

"I have a plan." Blue interrupted their conversations. "Will you keep Janet here just to be on the safe side?"

"If we keep her here, how will she meet with the strangers on the ferry as she was directed? So we can trap them."

"You would use her as a decoy!" Blue put a protective arm around her daughter.

CHAPTER TWENTY

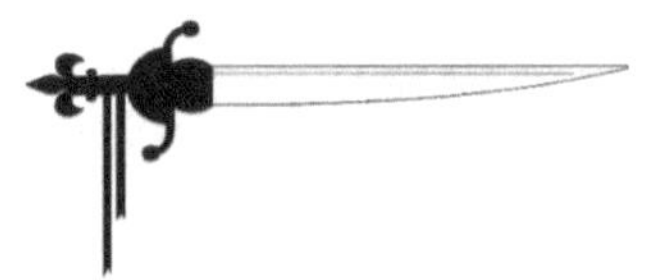

YOU MAKE ME SICK

I had the day off from school. Every month there was a prayer and meditation day. Half of us went one day, the other half the next day. The chapel was too small to accommodate us all. I called the Buccaneers and asked them to meet me at the *Foghorn*. I knew Sibby would be there because he had to finish the print run of the new edition.

"Let's see if we can make sense out of all this evidence," I said to Wing after executing the latest weird handshake of his, involving thumbs, elbows, and hand slapping. Leave it to Wing.

"Sibby, did you find out anything on Main?"

"Just that these guys Janet described have been seen hanging around the dock when shipments to Fred are loaded on the Alert or the cargo boat."

The press was noisy, and everyone was shouting to be heard. On top of that, the shortwave radio, a relic from when my dad worked for Fish and Wildlife, crackled in the background, giving off a high-pitched whine every now and then.

Mom was sorting the papers as Sibby cranked them out of the press, our beloved 1800's model. It worked and we couldn't afford a new one.

Blue Smoke appeared at the door and rattled the knob. Mom looked up and then at Sibby. She had been locking the door since the clubhouse burned.

"Oh, it Blue." She opened the door and Blue slipped into the room, closing it quickly, and peering out through the glass to see if anyone had followed her.

"Did you print my column yet," she demanded, a little out of breath. Her hair had come loose from her braid, and one shoe was missing a heel. Everyone in the room turned to look at her.

Mom looked at Sibby. "It was on page ten."

"No. That's the next page," he replied.

"Thank God," Blue said plopping down in the nearest chair.

"What's the matter?" Mom asked.

"Okay. I need you all to help me and Janet."

"I thought that's what we were doing," I chimed in. By then all the Buccaneers had arrived.

We listened as Blue spilled the beans. Now, it's all coming together. I looked at Wing and the others. Ratchet was clutching a big manilla envelope, hopefully full of her photos from the ferry.

"Where is Janet now?" Sibby asked.

"She's with Tim and Stella Walking Tree at the settlement, for now."

"Where's our money?" Snap demanded, getting to the heart of the matter.

"I'm afraid the men from the ferry have it," Blue told him. She turned to Becca. "I have an idea that might help us get these guys. I'd like to replace the old column you have with a new one I think might flush them out."

We gathered around Blue as she told us her plan.

"I've written a column warning the readers to avoid prescription medicines unless their doctors wrote a script for them. Remember, it looks like they want to set up their own drug store of prescription meds and have me sell them to my tribe members."

"Where do these drugs come from?" Mom asked.

"I've no idea, but I can't believe it's not some illegal source. Why else would they be threatening me and blackmailing Janet?"

"Is that what they call a black market?" Snap asked.

"What's black market?" Wing interrupted. "It's not a slavery thing, is it?" He grimaced.

"It's when you get a bunch of goods that folks can't get at regular stores or that cost too much at regular stores, and you sell them, either at higher prices if the demand is great, or at lower prices to outsell the regular stores. Lots of times the way you get the goods is not legal," Sibby explained.

"Oh," I said as the other Buccaneers nodded and grunted their understanding.

"I think they think we Injuns are just dumb," Blue said, dripping with sarcasm. "It's an old story but they just don't know us. It doesn't matter. What matters is that we stop this. Janet is in danger and so is everyone here."

"Do you have your new column," Mom asked.

"Right here." Blue handed Mom a typewritten sheet.

"I know how to set the type. You guys can help." I gestured to the Buccaneers who enthusiastically gathered around.

"Where's the page this goes on?"

Mom showed us the type-set page and together we picked out the letters from the old column. The Buccaneers were busy setting aside the letters that would type-set the new column. When all the old column was removed, we started filling in the frame with the letters that would put our plan in motion.

"Wow. This is so neat!" Ratchet was loving this new toy.

"You might even give up your camera for type-setting," I teased.

"Ready!" The Buccaneers yelled in unison.

Sibby picked up the page and loaded it into the press. He started cranking away. He inked and cranked, and we added this last page to the rest of the printed pages. Once all the pages were assembled, we folded them assembly-line procedure and bundled them into packages of twenty for delivery. The paper boys and girls would drop by for them at three o'clock, and a package would go to Main on the ferry at five.

"The ferry strangers are coming to meet with Janet tomorrow," Blue said.

"You're not letting her meet them!" Mom was outraged.

"I have to. To make this work."

Sibby stepped forward. "Listen, Blue. We'll all be there. We're all going to Main on the Five O'clock tomorrow. Right gang?"

"Yay!" the room erupted in whistles and cheers.

"AND. I'll be there with my camera. AND. By the way, don't you want to see the ones I already took?"

"I do," said Blue. Can I take them and show them to Tim Walking Tree? I want to see if he recognizes them as the same guys who were trying to break into my house."

"Sure." Ratchet handed the envelope to Blue.

"I want to see them too," I held out my hand to Blue.

We spread the photos on the table. "Any of you guys ever seen our suspects? Besides Ratchet?"

"I saw this one in church last Sunday," Snap said. "He was sorta looking around the whole building. I thought he was the construction man. The roof leaks and Father Felix was planning to fix it."

"And that was the day I gave the fund raiser money to Father Felix to hide in the vestry. I bet this man you identified overheard me," I said. "Speaking of Father Felix, should we invite him to our little ferry outing." I thought he should see what our missing money was all about.

Blue scooped the photos and slid them into the envelope. "Will we meet here tomorrow? Before the showdown at the ferry?"

I looked at Mom and Sibby.

"Yes, we need a plan of who does what." Sibby agreed and Mom seconded it.

"Everybody!" I gave a shrill whistle. "Let's make a plan."

You know how I love a plan.

CHAPTER TWENTY-ONE

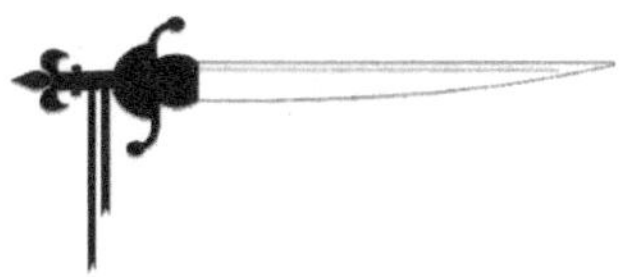

BRING IN THE MARINES

We Buccaneers decided to get to the ferry early and find places where we could observe but move quickly if we had to save Janet from the ferry men.

The time passed slowly. That might be how the theory of relativity works. It's all in your mind. When you want time to fly, it crawls. It only flies when you want something to last a long time. I am firmly convinced that Saturdays and Sundays are the shortest days of the week. Maybe Albert Einstein can shed some light on my observations. Sorry, off the topic again.

Wing and Ratchet were on the top of the ferry terminal building hiding behind the peaked façade on its front. The ticket taker, Jack, helped them, using a ladder allowing them to access a trap door leading to the roof. Wing was to help Ratchet load film as she needed it. Wing would also give a signal when he saw the strangers.

We had all memorized the faces of these bad guys from Ratchet's photos. Wing and Ratchet would see them first from their vantage point on the roof.

Snap and Bletch had Walkie-Talkies and would communicate with Red, the captain of the Alert. If something went wrong, she would keep the ferry at the dock.

I mean, what could go wrong? They could kidnap Janet. They could destroy evidence. We were hoping to get evidence of what they wanted Janet to do. We needed a witness to their conversation with her.

Sibby and Mom went to meet with Tim Walking Tree. It was 4:55 and still no Janet. I was getting nervous.

My job was to get on the ferry where I could get close to the men when they met with Janet and overhear their conversation. Then I was to follow the men when they got off at Main and see where they went, even getting a license number if they had a car. What if they grabbed Janet? What if they grabbed me? Then, what could I do?

4:59 and Janet came down the walk to the ferry dock. She was followed by two of the younger elders (I know, very confusing), who did their best not to appear to be with her.

That part of the plan was for the "elders" to use Red's short-wave radio to contact the tribal police on Main.

The Alert gently bumped along the pilings that helped guide it in and out of the slip and keep it there, especially if the wind was blowing. The passengers filed off. I watched for a signal from Wing but saw the bad guys myself as they stepped onto the dock. There were four of them. All wore hats that shielded their faces, and their jacket collars were turned up.

Janet walked up to them. They handed her a paper bag bound with string, about twelve inches square. She waved her hand at them in a gesture that said, "I don't want this." The tallest of the four put his hand in the pocket of his leather jacket.

I wish I could read lips. Janet was shaking her head and backing up. The second man in a blue windbreaker grabbed her elbow and pushed her toward the ferry.

I was so engrossed in watching this scene that I didn't notice the two young elders come up behind me. I felt a nudge in my back and nearly fainted. "Get on the ferry," the voice whispered. "We're right behind you," the other ordered.

Janet, wild-eyed and pulling away, glanced behind her. At the sight of the two elders a few passengers behind her, she calmed down and went with the four men.

Janet and her four captors took places at the Alert's railing. I did not like this. They could throw her overboard. I looked around for my two elders. They took seats near the railing in hearing distance of Janet and the captors.

The gate rattled shut behind us signaling the ferry would soon be pulling out of the slip. Just as the deck hands were about to cast off the heavy cables holding Alert to the dock, Red sounded the ferry's horn. The deck hands looked up at the wheelhouse and Red pointed to the passenger walkway.

I don't believe it.

Father Felix and Sister JoAnn hurried onto the ferry and Red tooted twice more. The lines were cast off and the ferry slipped the slip.

The captors were having an animated conversation with Janet. The elders edged forward, witnessing what they were saying. Janet clutched the package they had given her as if it contained a million dollars, or some very valuable evidence if our plan worked out.

How would we separate Janet from these men? What were they going to do with her? She was surrounded by friends who promised to save her. But what were we going to do?

CHAPTER TWENTY-TWO

DROWNED LIKE RATS

And then, what to my wonderment, Sister JoAnn and Father Felix walked over to Janet, eyeing the strangers.

"Janet! We've been looking all over for you. Who are these men? Are they friends of yours? Tribal members from another settlement?" Father Felix and Sister JoAnn turned to the men. They had no place to go. We had another half hour before we docked at Main.

Taking a cue from our clergy, I stepped up and approached Janet. "Hi, Janet. Going shopping on Main? Who are your friends?"

The two elders approached and greeted Janet. The men were surrounded. Their only option was to jump overboard.

The ferry lurched in a way I had never experienced. We were turning around!

Why was Red doing this? Had someone signaled her? Could it have been Snap and Bletch with the walkie-talkies? I don't know what the distance range is.

The men looked for a way out. They ran toward the exit, but we had not docked yet.

Sister JoAnn had her arm around a tear-streaked Janet. The two elders climbed to the wheelhouse where Red could be seen grabbing the short-wave radio mic and speaking into it.

Four loud splashes announced the strangers' escape. It was a truly dumb plan. The only place to swim to was the ferry dock or the rocky shore around it.

To the confusion of the ferry passengers, the Alert docked again. The elders elbowed their way around passengers, running to the ferry parking lot where a Tribal Police station wagon pulled in, doors flying open even before it stopped. Two officers got out and ran to the shore where the bad guys had to be dragged from the water, exhausted from trying to climb the rocks to get on shore.

The ferry passengers gawked as the soaked escapees were hand-cuffed and loaded into the Police station wagon to be taken back to headquarters and jail on Main. We didn't have a jail on Fred.

Janet, Father Felix, Sister JoAnn and I got off the ferry. I looked at Janet's surprise rescuers and said, "How did you know to confront Janet? You took an awful chance. I think one of those men with her had a gun."

"We didn't," replied Father Felix. "We were on our way to the Parish Education Office on Main when we saw Janet. We knew she was missing. It was the natural thing to do to help her out."

Blue's car rumbled into the parking lot. She and Tim emerged and ran to the elder elders who were emerging from their own station wagon. The younger elder patted Tim on the back and pointed at Janet who ran to her mother.

"What is this all about?" Sister JoAnn said, heaving a frustrated sigh.

"The short version, Sister," I said. "Those men were black-mailing Janet so she would convince her mother to sell their black-market drugs through her healing work here on Fred." Becca nodded, she and Sibby having come by to listen.

"Who's got the package those men gave to Janet?" I asked.

"It's here." Janet handed it to me. And digging in her pocket, she pulled out the one they had given her which was witnessed by Ratchet.

"Let me see what's in it." Blue pulled at the strings. Several bottles spilled out as Blue clutched them using the wrapping paper. "Penicillin and pain killers."

"What do the labels on the bottles say," Sibby asked.

"U.S. Army Medical Corps. These guys got the stuff, probably stolen, from either a field hospital or from all the unaccounted-for supplies that just kind of went missing as the War wound down. There were a lot of opportunities to make money from these supplies especially in the bombed-out cities in Europe and Asia. I'm surprised any of it made it home." Tim said.

"How do you know all this." Mom looked at Tim with renewed respect.

"I served in the Army during the War ya know, Becca, Army Intelligence."

"What should we do with it?" Blue asked.

"It's evidence against those four now. The Tribal Police have them in custody, so I'll give it to them. By the way, we're not to leave Fred, any of us. Someone will be contacting us to get our statements soon."

We said goodbye to Blue, Janet and Tim. Father Felix and Sister JoAnn had already gone, taking the rest of the Buccaneers with them. That could prove dangerous. I hope they don't give away any secrets. Sibby walked me, Wing and Mom home. The tribal elders were talking to the Tribal Police as we left.

Amid the barking and the leg rubbing from Fish as we arrived home, I asked Mom, "Do you think Blue's new column made a difference?"

"I don't know. We'll see what those men have to say," she replied, yawning.

The yawning was catching. I was suddenly very tired.

"Can you get your pals together tomorrow after school? The police are coming here to question us."

"Sure, Mom." I stifled another yawn. "I gotta go to bed now."

CHAPTER TWENTY-THREE

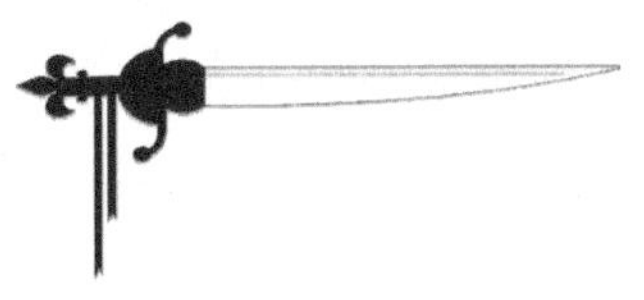

MEANWHILE . . .

Tim, Blue and Janet made it home in time to see the door slightly ajar. Tim was standing on the front steps.

"Tim. I'm so glad you are here." Blue stared. She looked at Tim. "I locked the door when I left."

"I know where you hide your key, and I checked to make sure no one was inside."

Blue Smoke made a quick check to see if their home had been robbed or vandalized. There was an envelope on the kitchen table with a note. "Did you leave this here, Tim?"

"Yes. Thought I'd surprise you. Sergeant Johnnie Rain said you must give it back, but I convinced him to let me borrow it for a few hours. I thought it would ease your mind."

When Blue Smoke picked up the fat envelope, money tumbled out, singles and fives and tens. "The Buccaneer's money!" she shouted.

Tim opened his arms and Janet flung herself into his embrace giving him a proper

hug. "Thank you, my wise elder. You saved me a second time today."

CHAPTER TWENTY-FOUR

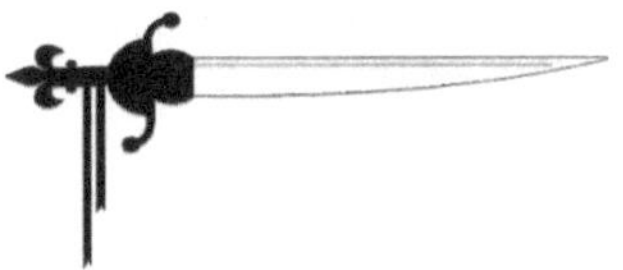

IT AIN'T OVER, TILL IT'S OVER

(YOGI BERRA)

Banging, barking, howling, footsteps clunking down the stairs. I woke up to all that racket, leaping to my feet and grabbing my soft ball bat. I crept to the head of the stairs to see what new danger faced us.

Did those four men come back for Mom and me? Shaking my sleep-fuzzy head, I remembered. They were arrested.

What I heard was Mom's voice and a deeper one I immediately recognized as Sibby's. I pulled on a sweatshirt and joined them in the kitchen.

"Lassie, you survived!"

"Arf," I replied. "Sibby, I just realized something. You weren't at the ferry yesterday. Where were you?"

"I was rounding up the Beachies in case you needed help," he explained.

"But you never showed up until the very end."

"We ran into the Tribal Police and they got the word on the short-wave radio that Sister JoAnn had the four villains in captivity."

"Well, you know she had a little help," I said.

Another knock at the door and Blue Smoke and Janet joined us.

"I have something for you, Lily. But you can't keep it."

She handed me a fat envelope. "The money!" I shouted. "Why can't I keep it?"

Is this what's meant by an Indian giver? I chuckled to myself.

"Evidence," said Janet. "I . . .I . . .I was so scared. I'm sorry, Lily."

"I'm sorry too. We could've helped you if you had just trusted someone."

Janet nodded. "I'll try," she whispered looking at Blue Smoke.

"Janet, can you clear up some things for us?"

She looked at me, brows raised in question, "Sure."

"You were in the cave. We found your stuff,"

"Yeah."

"We heard moaning and clicking. Did you hear that too? What was that?"

She chuckled. "I was there when you guys had your meeting. My flashlight died when I was leaving through the tunnel and I kept slapping it on my hand and mumbling at it. That must've been what you heard."

"So, you know about the other rooms in the cave and the tunnels."

"I like to explore. I figured if this was Jon Buccleigh's cave, it probably had access to the bay. And I found it!"

"Pretty dangerous to do it alone," Sibby said.

"I didn't think so. The walls and ceiling all seemed pretty solid. There were no piles of rocks looking like there'd been rockslides."

"You are one lucky kid," Sibby said.

Janet blushed looking at her shoes.

"One other thing," I said. "One of the beachies thinks he saw you in our burned-out clubhouse with a box. Was that you? And what was the box?"

"It was me. It was just my stuff that I was hiding in the cave. I went to the clubhouse to see if I could find out why it burned."

"Why didn't you just ask somebody," Sibby said.

"I was the one who stole the money. I didn't feel like I could just ask one of you. Guilt, I suppose."

Wingnut burst through the door followed by a jabbering Ratchet, Bletch and Snap hot on their heels. The kitchen was getting crowded.

Sibby got up and with a wink at Mom, banged his fist on the table.

Ever so subtle, I thought.

When the china stopped trembling and jangling, he cleared his throat. "I would like the Buccaneers to accompany me to a meeting of the Beachies. And Mrs. Dawes please come as our honored guest."

I looked at the other Buccaneers. They looked at me and each other.

"Let's see what can be done about your clubhouse," Sibby said, responding to our silence at his invitation.

"Sure," I said, shrugging my shoulders, followed by similar gestures from the Buccaneers.

Sibby nodded solemnly, sweeping a gallant gesture toward Mom and the door, and we left.

It was a clear and sunny morning. We get those sometimes in October. In the distance the blackened remains of our clubhouse stood out against the bluest of skies.

"I hope those guys get charged with arson. They could have killed someone." Mom said.

"Yup. One of the Beachies could've been squatting there that night," Sibby added.

"Or it could have been Janet. Those nights she didn't go home," said Wing and muttered, "Could've been me one of those nights I slipped out."

"Oh. By the way, those cigarette butts I collected belonged to Sunny. He sometimes just hangs out wherever he feels safe."

Just beyond the Buccaneers' Headquarters, as I liked to call our clubhouse, a crowd had gathered. The Beachies! All standing close together and talking excitedly with each other.

As we approached, they parted, revealing a new addition to the collection of huts that formed their colony,

"Where'd that come from?"

The Beachies broke into "For He's a Jolly Good Fellow".

"What the heck," Snap said mouth hanging open. "It's your clubhouse," Sibby said. "Take a look. Give it a name."

A new chant arose from the crowd. "Buccaneers. Buccaneers. Three cheers for Buccaneers!"

****

So, there it was. Whatever happened to me in my life, that singular adventure that I've told you about was the sweetest, the best. And it happened on St. Frederick Island in 1947.

AFTERWARD

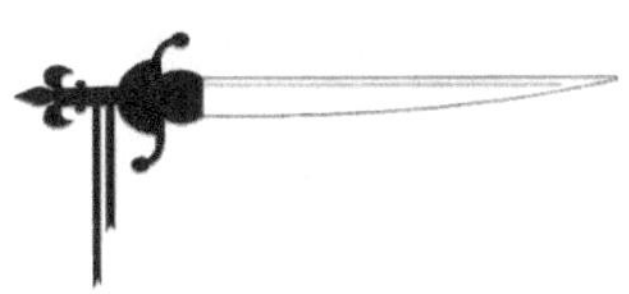

Janet was made a Buccaneer before the end of the school year. Tabitha Blue Smoke's clinic in the school was opened to all the residents of Fred. The Tribes reciprocated by opening the Long House to all the residents of Fred to explore Native American lore, medicines, and traditional crafts.

Sister Superior opened a preschool/daycare for all Freds.

The *Foghorn* not only flourished on Fred but picked up a following on Main.

Sibby came to dinner every Sunday, and eventually the *Foghorn* got a new press.

All of us Buccaneers switched to the high school on Main. I will always remember those ferry rides on the Alert, fog swirling around us and Frank Sinatra singing "Time after Time" on Red Winterberry's short-wave radio.

The Buccaneers graduated and while some stayed on Fred to serve the community that nurtured them, others went on to live on Main and beyond.

Sprocket, that's me, went on to teach science at Main High School.

Linda Maria Frank, retired from a career teaching science, including forensic science, resides on Long Island and is currently writing the Annie Tillery Mysteries, <u>The Madonna Ghost</u>, <u>Girl with Pencil, Drawing</u>, <u>Secrets in the Fairy Chimneys</u> and <u>The Mystery of the Lost Avenger</u>. She also produces <u>The Writer's Dream</u>, her local access TV show, seen on YouTube. Frank is active in LI Authors Group, LI Sisters in Crime, LI Children's Writers and Illustrators, and Mystery Writers of America.

Linda does lectures on Topics on Forensic Science at libraries, universities, clubs and other venues.

She has a by-line in LifeStyles 50+ Magazine, The Authors Corner.